8/24

THE HATCH DOOR SWUNG OPEN TO REVEAL THE VASTEST stretch of our ship, towering four stories high and packed from floor to ceiling with rows upon rows of cargo, all sealed in white compartments built into the walls. Attached to one of those walls would be a seven-foot-tall, dish-shaped antenna. It was the focal point of the room, the home base of our comm system.

Except . . . it was gone.

ALEXANDRA MONIR

THE
LIFE
BELOW

THE SEQUEL TO *THE FINAL SIX*

HARPER TEEN
An Imprint of HarperCollinsPublishers

HarperTeen is an imprint of HarperCollins Publishers.

Library of Congress Control Number: 2019951567
ISBN 978-0-06-265898-2 (pbk.)

Typography by Heather Daugherty
20 21 22 23 24 PC/LSCH   10 9 8 7 6 5 4 3 2 1
❖
First paperback edition, 2021

For Chris and Leo,

My world and my stars.

PART ONE

EARTH

PROLOGUE

PONTUS to EARTH Live Blog

DAY 43

Astronaut: ARDALAN, NAOMI

[Message Status: Upload Failure]

Some disasters begin with a warning, an iceberg you can spot from miles ahead. Others come on all at once, as violent as they are quick, like the earthquakes and hurricanes that wrecked us back home. But up here, it's easy to miss the trigger altogether. A wire doesn't make a sound when it snaps. You don't know what's happened until after—when the creeping sense of dread moves beyond your body and takes the form of a flawed ship.

I don't think I've ever felt so helpless as I do now, writing to an entire population that will never see these words. We're going dark and you won't know why or what it means, but you'll assume the worst. And that's what has me wide-awake and clammy with sweat in the middle of the night, afraid that if I open my mouth I'll

1

start screaming and never stop.

I can't live with them thinking I'm dead. Just imagining my parents and Sam holding each other in grief at a memorial ceremony, staring at my photo while mourners recite Rūmī, hurts worse than any physical pain. And Leo . . . what will he do when he hears the news? When my emails and video messages come to a sudden halt, how will he react? How will *I* make it through losing the four of them? I used to think communicating through a computer screen would never be enough, but now it seems like the ultimate privilege. One that I'd give anything to have back.

Maybe that's why I'm writing now, even as logic tells me it's hopeless. I have to keep trying, on the off chance that I might press Submit and, this time, hear the whoosh of delivery. The sound of everything returning to normal. Or at least as close to it as "normal" can be up here.

We'd been traveling through space for just forty-two days, three hours, and twelve minutes when it happened. It was seven in the morning, Coordinated Universal Time, and the first thing I noticed when I woke up was the sound of silence. Normally, NASA Mission Control serves as our alarm clock, waking us up at the same time each morning by piping a song through the cabin speakers. You could count on them to choose something on-brand and space-themed, like yesterday's vintage Coldplay track, "A Sky Full of Stars." But today there was no song at all. Someone must have fallen asleep on the job. Still, I woke up on cue.

We had half an hour to ourselves before we were due in the dining room for breakfast, and over the past few days I'd figured out how to get ready in ten minutes or less. This way, I could start the day in my favorite part of the ship—the one place where I never felt claustrophobic, or desperate to claw my way out.

I climbed out of my bunk and slipped off my favorite flannel pajamas, which somehow still retained the faintest smell of home. Then I stepped into the tiny shower stall attached to my cabin, which flashed a green light as soon as my feet hit the floor. A timer began, reminding me that the water would shut off in three minutes. Our entire existence here on the *Pontus* seemed to be dominated by countdown clocks.

After squeezing a dollop of shampoo onto my head and rinsing as frantically as someone with a lice problem, the shower was over. I toweled off and threw on a pair of gray track pants and a peach hoodie, then slid open the door of my cabin to the common room. Usually at least one or two of us could be found in here before breakfast, reading or watching TV, but it was empty this morning.

I jogged through the long module that makes up our crew quarters and rode the elevator pod down to the main hatch, leaving the artificial gravity behind. From there I floated, into a place that comforted and intimidated me in equal measure.

The Observatory is a circular chamber made up of wall-to-wall, indestructible quartz-glass windows, which gives you the illusion of flying untethered through the universe. It's the high of a spacewalk, minus the danger. The darkness surrounds you on all sides, with a sudden sweep of beauty whenever the ship spirals within view of Earth. This was one of those mornings when I got to see the shock of color—the blue marble of home.

I pressed my palms against the glass, staring in awe. Somewhere on that planet, in a time zone eight hours behind ours, my parents and brother were just now falling asleep for the night, while six thousand miles from them, Leo was waking up and starting his day. I closed my eyes, trying to picture his surroundings, what that day would look like. And that's when the pain socked me in the stomach. *We don't exist in the same world anymore.*

I took a few breaths to steady myself, stopping the tears before they had a chance to start. I turned away from the blue, keeping my gaze fixed on the darkness and trying to pinpoint the stars around me, until it was time to join the others. When I crawled back through the hatch, I found someone waiting for me on the other side.

Jian Soo, crewmate and copilot of our mission, glanced up sharply as I tumbled back into gravity.

"Morning," I greeted him. "You okay?"

He shook his head, his eyes frantic.

"Communication's down. Our flight nav software is still working fine, but I can't get any response from Houston. And then Sydney told me she tried logging on to email and kept getting an error message that said no connection found." He looked at me intently. "You can fix it, right?"

My first thought was that it was a joke. He was just pulling a prank—probably Beckett Wolfe's idea—to see how fast they could get a panic attack out of me. But then I remembered who I was talking to. Jian was the honest, solid, *good* one among us. And as I thought of the quiet this morning, the forgotten alarm from Mission Control, my stomach plunged.

"It—it has to be just a hiccup," I said, forcing myself to stay calm. "Let me go take a look."

That was my job, to run all the tech and communications on the ship. It had been easy enough until today, but this was uncharted territory. The *Pontus* was never supposed to lose its connection, not for a millisecond. It was as vital to the ship as oxygen.

I sprinted past Jian, toward the Communications Bay and its array of computers, where I found each screen flashing the same message in bold red letters.

COMMUNICATION SIGNALS DROPPED—NO CONNECTION FOUND.

"Houston." My voice came out like a whisper, but it didn't matter. No one could hear me anymore. "Houston, we're experiencing a comm failure. I'm rebooting the systems and running diagnostics, and will wait for further instructions from Mission Control."

By the time the computers powered back on after the reboot, my anxiety had grown into full-fledged panic. The dreaded words returned on-screen—*NO CONNECTION FOUND*—and my fingers shook as I ran a diagnostics scan, praying the answer would flash in front of me with a simple solution. Within minutes, the problem was staring me in the face. But it was the opposite of simple.

It was our X-band antenna. The single piece of equipment on this ship that enabled all our communication with Earth wasn't even *registering* on the equipment scan. It was as if the antenna never existed.

Something was bubbling in my stomach, a nausea-inducing fear, but I forced myself to stay focused and keep moving. I raced out of the Communications Bay and back to the hatch, where Jian was now joined by Sydney and Dev, the three of them looking almost as rattled as I felt. They turned to me expectantly, but all I could do was shake my head.

"I'm going to the payload bay. Something's up with the antenna."

"Should we go with you?" Dev offered.

"One of you, maybe. There's not room for much more. But we've got to hurry."

I yanked open the hatch door and climbed inside, with Dev right behind me. We crawled and then floated our way through two different tunnel passageways, known as nodes, until we reached the center of the ship. The payload bay required a password to enter, which always struck me as odd—was a break-in really such a risk when we were the only six humans for hundreds of millions of miles? It took Dev and me ten minutes of racking our brains and scrolling through the notes on our wrist monitors before we finally cracked it.

The hatch door swung open to reveal the vastest stretch of our ship, towering four stories high and packed from floor to ceiling with rows upon rows of cargo, all sealed in white compartments built into the walls. Attached to one of those walls would be a seven-foot-tall, dish-shaped antenna. It was the focal point of the room, the home base of our comm system.

Except . . . it was gone.

The thumping in my chest tripled in speed, loud enough for me to hear the frenetic beating through my headset. I stared at the giant empty space overwhelming the room, half convinced I was hallucinating. It wouldn't be the first time an astronaut lost their grip on reality.

"Tell me—how does the biggest, most powerful

antenna of its kind just up and *disappear*?"

"It doesn't," Dev says, all color draining from his face. "Someone made it disappear."

I followed his gaze and that's when I saw the loose bolt, drifting toward us from the back of the module. It was one of the same bolts used to secure the antenna, only this one was floating free—and heavy enough to kill us with a single strike.

"Move!" I screamed, grabbing Dev's arm and pulling him away just before the bolt careened into our path. We each seized one of the handrails running up the length of the wall, swinging from one to the next like amateur rock climbers in zero g. My head brushed the ceiling as we reached the top story, a safe distance from the floating weapon below. I looked down at the damaged payload bay in disbelief.

"Someone *did this* to us. Someone actually snuck in here, unscrewed the bolts, dismantled the antenna, and . . ."

My eyes caught on the payload door, fused into the opposite wall. It wasn't supposed to open for months— not until the Europa landing. But clearly somebody had opened it, and pushed the antenna through to disappear in space. "Someone wanted us cut off and isolated from the entire world," I whispered, fighting the bile rising in my throat. "Why?"

"Not just someone," Dev said, swallowing hard. "One of us."

It was like every star in the universe gave out at once, plunging us into an empty, pitch-dark world.

We were lost to Earth. And we were trapped, hurtling through space at thirty thousand miles an hour, with an enemy far more dangerous than we could have imagined.

SIX WEEKS EARLIER . . .

ONE

LEO

WHEN SHE LEFT, IT WAS LIKE THE SUN SLIPPED FROM THE UNI-verse. I watched the Earth turn dark, cold, and bleak, right in front of me on live TV.

I thought I knew my way around loneliness—how to swallow the sting, push away memories, ignore the silence. But nothing prepares you for this: watching a spacecraft launch into the sky, with the person you love inside.

The live feed on-screen holds me captive, showing the Final Six strapped into their launch seats, their bodies now shuddering with the second engine burn. Naomi reaches out a gloved hand, and though Sydney Pearle is the one to grasp it, I know who she was really reaching for.

Outside the ship's windows, I can see the colors begin to change. The pale blue sky is receding, taking its final bow. And then, quick as a breath—blue turns to black. The stuffed ladybug hanging from the ceiling, NASA's lucky talisman, starts to float.

The Final Six are officially in space.

The newscasters narrating every step of the journey erupt in applause, losing their "serious" voices as they shriek and cheer. I wish I could share in their joy, but the closest I come is relief, followed by another wave of longing. The same desperate pull that brought me here to Vienna, where I'm now standing beside a silver-haired tech mogul who calmly says, "Glad to see that went off without a hitch," before returning to her desk. The sound of Dr. Wagner's voice brings me back to the moment—the reason I'm here. *My second chance.*

"How soon can we launch?" I call after her, my eyes still glued to the TV.

"No later than next week. We need to make sure you depart while Mars is orbiting forty-four degrees ahead of Earth's rotation, in order for our spacecraft to arrive at the correct time and position to dock with the *Pontus*. Since we're already in the midst of this target alignment window now, I'm afraid we don't have much of a time allowance if you're going to catch up to the Final Six."

I turn to face Dr. Greta Wagner, the scientist, inventor, and billionaire handing me my last hope. We're in the middle of a conference room in the Wagner Enterprises compound, a modernist palace of slate and steel, with exterior walls rising high to keep out prying eyes. While Greta flips through a massive mission binder spread across the conference table, an assistant hovers over her shoulder, tapping away at a blinking tablet. Meanwhile, the humanoid robot she introduced as her butler, Corion, rolls in and out, delivering messages and replenishing Dr. Wagner's never-ending cups of black coffee. We're two days into my stay, and still none of this feels . . . real.

"I know it's a tall order, expecting you to be ready this quickly," Greta continues. "But once you reach orbit, the ship will fly itself on autopilot, right up until you attempt docking with the *Pontus* at Mars. I've designed the *Wagner-One*, and your mission itself, to be as user-friendly and foolproof as possible. I've also called in some reinforcements to help with your training. We may only have a week together, but it will be a week of monumental growth and preparation." She pauses. "It has to be."

"Right." I nod, trying to block out the creeping thoughts of how utterly alone I'll be up there. I'll be skating the line between life and death the entire time. But no matter how daunting, this is what I wanted. It's what I asked for.

"Before we begin . . ." She slides a sheaf of papers across the table toward me. "I need you to sign this. Take your time reading it through. I had it printed in both English and Italian."

I glance down at the top page, where the words jump out at me in bold black ink.

I, Leonardo Danieli, being of sound mind, free will, and legal age, hereby declare that I willingly accept the position of Sole Astronaut & Commander on the WagnerOne Mission to Europa, a private venture. I understand that any private space travel unsanctioned by the government is against the laws of the Outer Space Treaty, and as such, I am entitled to no protection or resources from any of the space agencies. I accept that this is a one-way trip, and that the mission could result in my death should it fail. I am aware of all of the above facts, and remain committed as ever to the mission and the privilege of colonizing Europa. I release Dr. Greta Wagner and the entirety of Wagner Enterprises from any future claim or liability therein.

"You know I have no one left, right? No one who would care enough to—to sue you if I die?" I try to joke over my speeding heartbeat.

Greta doesn't crack a smile.

"There are always people on the periphery who come forward when they sense money to be gained. And once the world finds out where you are, the ISTC and NASA will try to spin it as me forcing you to do my bidding. This signed waiver and our witness"—she nods at her assistant—"will protect us both."

I'm not sure how any of it protects me, but I don't bother asking. My attention is drawn back to the screen, where the Final Six are unbuckling from their seats. Their first moments of weightlessness bring gasps and nervous laughter, and then they are floating as a group toward the airlock. But Naomi deviates from the rest, stopping at one of the windows to press her gloves against the glass and look down at Earth. The ache spreads from my chest, the pain of something breaking.

At the airlock door, Dev Khanna turns the handle and the hatch swings open. The frame freezes, and after a torturous moment of static, the livestream shifts to the crew quarters—the Final Six's new home, from now to Europa.

When the six reappear on-screen, they've changed out of their spaceflight suits and into matching silver *Mission: Europa* jackets over polo shirts bearing their country's space agency logo. Only two share the same logo: Naomi and Beckett Wolfe. I watch Beckett brush against Naomi's shoulder as they float through the module, and it's like a punch in my stomach.

I turn away and grab a pen off the conference table. I don't need to read another word of this contract; I'm signing. But Greta places a hand on my arm just before I scrawl my name.

"I need to know that you understand what it is you're signing up for."

Something in her expression gives me pause.

"What do you mean? Why would I change my mind?"

"Because a solo mission to space is one of the greatest challenges a human being can endure. You will experience many moments of profound loneliness and fear. Are you ready for that?"

"I would be alone on Earth, too," I remind her. "With my family gone, and now Naomi . . . What difference does it make whether I'm alone down here or up there?"

"There is one key difference," she says. "By sending you to space without government approval, you'll be committing a crime—both of us will. In the long run, after you help the Final Six survive, as I know you—*we*—can, you'll be seen as a hero. But in the short term, the people you leave behind on Earth will view you and me both as reckless criminals. Maybe even saboteurs." She hesitates. "You might not find such a welcoming reception from the Final Six when you first arrive, either."

The thought stops me cold—traveling all that way through space, only to find that she never wanted me there in the first place.

"And while I will do everything in my power to keep you safe up there," she continues, "I can't promise that Dr. Takumi and General Sokolov won't try retaliating through their own resources in space."

I swallow hard, my throat like sandpaper. I can't deny that she's managed to shake me.

"It feels like you're trying to talk me out of this. Why?"

"No. I'm making sure of my choice," she says, eyeing me carefully. "It's my responsibility to discuss these worst-case scenarios with you, since we both have to know: How far are you willing to go for the Final Six? For the future of humankind?"

I look back at the screen, where the six are floating out of another hatch and into the Habitation Module, an artificial-gravity zone containing their sleeping cabins and common areas. One minute they're skimming the ceiling, and the next, their feet hit the ground. Yet another wonder of the *Pontus*.

"Before I answer that, there's something I need to know too." I lock eyes with Greta. "What did you mean when you said that only you and I can provide the help the Final Six needs? What is your plan for Europa?"

I can almost see the wheels turning in Greta's mind as she mulls over what to tell me. And then—

"I'll show you."

MESSAGE ORIGIN: EARTH—UNITED STATES—
SOUTHWEST TEXAS
MESSAGE RECIPIENT: *PONTUS* SPACECRAFT—
EARTH ORBIT
ATTN: ARDALAN, NAOMI
[MESSAGE STATUS: RECEIVED—ENCRYPTED]

Hey, Sis.

I've tried writing this email three times already, and I can't seem to land on the right words. I thought I'd start with some jokes to make you smile, but let's face it, I don't exactly kill when it comes to comedy. So I scrapped that and told you what it was *really* like to leave the launchpad after we all said good-bye. That email was about as uplifting as classic Russian literature, so I hit Delete again. Now here I am just trying to be normal, when our lives have diverged so far from that.

I thought a lot of things might happen to us—I thought I might not live long enough to see them—but I never predicted this. Losing my sister. And I know, I know, I'm not really losing you. Not completely. But when it's just me and our parents, and when we go back home and your room stays empty—well, it sure feels that way.

Anyway. The truth is, hard as this is, I am so proud of you. We all are. Mom keeps burning *esfand* in our hotel room to ward off the evil eye, since everywhere we go, people are raving about you. How your bravery and smarts could make the mission a real success, and save the rest of us from dying out on this hostile Earth. (No pressure or anything!)

Tomorrow the ISTC jet flies us home to LA, where we've been told things should be a little different. As some sort of compensation for your "services to the global cause," the US government and the United Nations are covering some of our expenses, like my cardiologist bills and heart medications, which I knew you'd be relieved to hear about—*and* a monthly delivery of unrationed groceries! They even offered to move us to a flood-safe house to live rent-free, but Mom and Dad refused that on the spot. None of us want to leave the last place you lived. So they negotiated a deal where the government covers three-quarters of the rent, which should make a huge difference. They won't have to pull so many hours at work, and I won't feel like such an expensive burden. You've helped us already, Sis.

So now it's my turn to help you. I've gotten pretty good at Python since you've been away, and I coded a site where we can transmit encrypted data back and forth. If you can send the data you found on Europa over to the domain address linked here, then I can put in the research time that I'm guessing you can't, under all that supervision. And then, hopefully, I can fill in some of the gaps.

For extra security, the site knows only one language:

Farsi. (Wish I could tell Mom and Dad! Remember how they had to literally *drag* us to Farsi school?) And I coded the landing page to redirect to a wormhole-theory blog, so anyone at NASA tracking your online habits will just think you've got another nerdy obsession. ;)

All right, someone's at the door—I think it's time for the farewell dinner they're hosting for the families of the Final Six. Which reminds me: yesterday I asked some ISTC staff how I could get in touch with your friend Leo, and they gave me nothing. But later, Dr. Takumi said to come by his office before I leave, so maybe he is planning to share Leo's contact info then. I'll keep you posted.

Stay safe up there. We love you.

S

TWO

NAOMI

THE VIEW IS WHAT MAKES IT REAL. I COULD ALMOST PRETEND, during liftoff, that I was simply on the most terrifying roller-coaster ride of my life, squeezing my eyes shut and freezing my emotions cold for those eight and a half minutes. But now we're here, well above the stratosphere—and with the sounds of celebration bursting through my earpiece, I have no choice but to look.

I unlatch my safety strap, and my body begins to rise. The feeling of weightlessness is a heady rush, like swimming with no water. I float toward the cockpit's cupola window, bumping and jostling against my crewmates along the way, as the six of us fumble through the first minutes of zero gravity. It doesn't matter that we practiced this half a dozen times in the Vomit Comet at space camp—everything becomes trickier once it's real.

I gaze out the window, and the sight sends goose bumps crawling across my skin. It's like I've woken up inside one of the posters that used to hang on my wall as a kid, with the all-encompassing darkness, the silver specks of stars peeking through the black. And then, just below our ship, I see the massive curve of blue and white, shielded by nothing but the thin, glowing ring of the atmosphere. Earth looks so fragile, so defenseless from up here. And suddenly, everything I've bottled inside rises to the surface. A sob lodges in my throat, a wave of grief so intense that for a second, I can't breathe. Until a familiar voice shakes me out of my thoughts.

"Well done, crew! Congratulations on a successful launch."

It's General Sokolov, our commander on the ground, speaking to us from Houston's Mission Control.

"Your loved ones and the public back home are all thrilled to see you achieve this critical first step in our mission," she continues, sounding uncharacteristically delighted. "Once you reached 330,000 feet, the *Pontus* Habitation Module attached to our booster inflated automatically to its full size. Your home in space is now open, and accessible through the airlock. Aside from Jian Soo and, of course, Cyb, the rest of you won't be seeing this flight capsule again until Mars."

I glance across the capsule at each of my crewmates, wondering if any of them feels the way I do—this growing sense of panic as we cut our ties to Earth—or if they're all just thrilled to be getting away, escaping our dying planet before it kills us too. It's impossible to guess what the others are thinking, when I barely know all but one of them . . . the same person I wish I'd never met.

Beckett Wolfe hovers near me, steadying himself on a handrail, and I inch away from him, gripping the back of one of the launch seats to keep my body from drifting. I know what he's capable of, how he wouldn't flinch before sabotaging any one of us—just like he did to Leo. And as I glance at him now, my nausea returns. His face just *rests* in a smug expression, like someone whose daily life consists of getting his way. I guess that's the perk of being rich and power-adjacent, the privileged nephew of Mr. President.

"You may now leave your space suits to charge in the airlock, and then go straight to the Communications Bay, where you will find another message from me and Dr. Takumi," the general instructs us. "Copy?"

"Roger that," Dev, our lieutenant commander, answers. He motions us forward and we follow him to the airlock, with only Cyb staying behind to man the cockpit. Before disappearing through the metal door, I turn to give the capsule one more look—the last place where I got to feel Earth beneath me.

The six of us each step into the space suit charging pods lining the airlock, which use mechanical claws to peel the heavy fabric off of us. I can hear the charging pods gurgling and humming behind us as we crawl out of the airlock through the hatch door, into the body of the ship.

We float through the tunnel-like hatch until we reach the Habitation Module, where our feet land with a *thunk* on the white-painted floor. It's the moment that gives me my first real smile in space. The design is genius: an artificial-gravity environment created by turning the module into an ever-rotating centrifuge. It's the work of my hero, Dr. Greta Wagner, and for the umpteenth time, I wonder *what* could have happened to get such a crucial figure fired from our mission.

We pass more tech wizardry on our way to the main crew quarters, from a triple-sealed solar storm shelter to an artificial greenhouse, where lettuce leaves and would-be plants grow like preemies in an incubator. And then, we arrive at the Astronauts' Residence.

My mouth falls open as we step onto the first floor, looking up at a soaring atrium surrounded by six wrap-around levels of living space. At the center of the atrium is a transparent, silver-glowing pod, to zip us up and down each floor, while a ceiling window gives us a constant view of the stars.

"Whoa," Sydney murmurs, echoing my thoughts.

"This definitely beats the mock-ups from space camp," Jian says.

Looking around, it's clear we're standing in the Communications Bay. Three blinking touch-screen desks are bolted to the floor along with matching white swivel chairs, while a 5K-HD screen covering nearly an entire wall displays a slideshow of well-wishers from around the world, cheering us on. Moments after we enter, a red light flickers overhead, followed by an audible click. I glance up and find a camera burrowed into the wall a few inches above my head, its lens pointed straight at me.

"We're being watched already," I say with the familiar twinge of discomfort that I know well from space camp. There is something so . . . so borderline *creepy* about being on camera twenty-four/seven. It's the reality show I never meant to sign up for, broadcast to all of Earth.

"They don't have these in our bed-and-baths, do they?" Minka Palladin, our crewmate from Ukraine, asks. She folds her arms over her chest, giving the camera a suspicious look.

"Certainly not."

We all jump as a familiar face fills the screen. Magnified in close-up, his features look almost exaggerated: fierce dark eyes under thick black brows, deep crevices in the skin where age has left its mark. Dr. Takumi is a jarring transition from the slideshow that was playing just moments ago. He fixes his piercing gaze on us through the screen, and then breaks into a smile. It makes him look like someone else—someone who might still have a heart. But I know better.

"Welcome, our chosen six, to space!" Dr. Takumi draws out the words for grand effect. "Tell me, how does it feel?"

We answer with a smattering of mumbles—"amazing,"

"weird," "exciting," "trippy"—while Beckett yells out, "Effing fan-*tas*-tic!" I roll my eyes at him, brownnosing the boss even from up here.

"Good." Dr. Takumi nods and the camera pans out to reveal him at his throne-like desk on ISTC campus, with General Sokolov standing at his shoulder. They are dressed in their respective uniforms, the black and red colors I've come to associate with them: black for Dr. Takumi's suit with an ISTC logo glowing at the chest, and red for the general's Roscosmos flight jacket and army pants.

"Now, you have a fair amount of time before your first stop in Mars orbit and the final destination of Europa, but these months en route will be far from idle," Dr. Takumi continues. "You have a spacecraft to protect, an artificial crop source to grow, and further training to complete for your new life on a new moon. And of course, the first leg of your trip will require the utmost precision and focus, with course corrections along the way as we monitor the fuel leak on the Mars supply ship."

My stomach sinks at the reminder of this wrench in the plan. The only way we'll have enough food and support systems for a lifetime on Europa is by collecting those materials from the supply ship that's currently on a never-ending loop around Mars, where it's been stuck in purgatory since the failed *Athena* mission five years ago. But when SatCon discovered the fuel leak, right before we all touched down at Space Training Camp, we learned that this cache of supplies we'd been counting on to survive is in jeopardy—because each day of dripping fuel sends the vessel ever so slightly out of alignment. If it slips outside of the *Pontus*'s trajectory, we could miss it altogether, and if it falls out of orbit before we get there . . . well, both scenarios would leave us starving to death. So, *everything* is riding on us making it in time for the Mars rendezvous and docking with the supply ship before it's lost to us forever. Not exactly a light task.

"Dr. Takumi and I will be actively involved every step of the way, watching and monitoring your progress and conducting your training from the ground," General Sokolov chimes in. "So if you've had any fears about the six of you being alone up there, with all that's at stake, just remember that we will continue to serve as your leaders every day through this process."

I hear Minka exhale and I catch Dev grinning at the screen in relief, but unlike my crewmates, the *last* thing I want is for the ISTC heads to remain omnipresent. Watching them hold sway over our team from behind the camera reminds me that we are at the mercy of this secretive, powerful pair.

"But," the general adds, "our involvement can only extend up to a point."

I stop short as her tone changes.

"Because the farther you travel from Earth, the longer the time delay in our communication. As you approach Mars, you can expect a four- to ten-minute gap each way between sending and receiving messages from the *Pontus* to Earth, and vice versa. The closer you get to Jupiter, the delay increases to roughly forty minutes each way."

I nod impatiently; they're not telling me anything I don't already know. The time delay was always one of my chief reservations about this mission. I mean, how helpful was an SOS signal when you had to wait as long as *eighty minutes* for a reply? We could all be dead in half the time it took to get a response. That's supposedly why the ISTC included two robots on our mission, superior AIs programmed to trouble-shoot almost any crisis. And then, in a flash, I remember my conversation on Air Force One, the words I couldn't stand to hear. Is the general's announcement about . . . that?

"Since quite a lot can happen in such a time frame, especially with the aforementioned Mars maneuver, one of you will assume the leadership role in our place, whenever Dr. Takumi and I are unreachable," she reveals. "During those hours, however long they last, five of you will follow the commands of your de facto leader—a person we are entrusting to make the right decisions by all of you."

Here it comes. I brace myself for the inevitable.

"Wait a sec," Sydney interjects. "Isn't that Cyb's job, to be proxy commander?"

"From a piloting and navigational standpoint, yes. But when it comes to the six of you, with any human decisions that need to be made, the final word rests with . . ."

I swallow hard, glaring at the floor.

"Beckett Wolfe."

"*What?*" Dev and Sydney both blurt out in unison, while Jian's expression turns thunderstruck. Beckett's eyes flit across each of us, a smile playing on his face. It's all I can do to not lunge at him, and wipe that smile off.

"Excuse me," Dev says with a cough. "I'm just wondering if that—I mean, that's a mistake, right? Because you and Dr. Takumi named me lieutenant commander before we left, and that outranks Beckett as underwater specialist—"

"As does copilot," Jian jumps in, hands balling into fists at his sides. Now that we're a world away, it seems no one is afraid to stand up to our leaders anymore.

The general frowns her disapproval at the two of them.

"I certainly shouldn't need to explain this. The copilot is chiefly concerned with assisting Cyb on the flight deck, while lieutenant commander means serving as the right hand to whomever *we* choose to lead," she says crisply. "In our absence, that will mean Beckett."

Dev looks repulsed, and I'm slightly gratified to see that I'm not the only one who feels this way about my fellow American. The thought of him having any power over me makes me ill, and more than that, it makes no sense. What sway does he hold over Takumi and Sokolov, and why?

"Why do we even need one person among us calling the shots, anyway?" I speak up. "Can't we just agree on things as a group, give everyone an equal voice?"

"That's the kind of thinking that'll get us stuck playing rock-paper-scissors when a crisis hits," Beckett scoffs. "You ever tried settling a vote with an even number of people?"

"Yeah, well it's a lot more appealing than you playing dictator—"

I break off midsentence as a black sheet of darkness falls over the room, eclipsing everything but Dr. Takumi's flashing eyes on-screen. And then I hear the deafening sound of scraping metal as walls that I didn't know existed slide in and around us. Our "home" is closing in on itself, shutting out all hatch openings—trapping us into this one module.

A scream echoes, and footsteps clatter as we stumble through the darkness. My heart is clanging in my chest as I feel my way around the walls, searching for another light source. And then—

There's the hum of electronics as the lighting powers back on, a whirring noise as the metal walls retreat. I look into the faces of four equally panicked crewmates, and up at the triumphant expressions of Dr. Takumi and General Sokolov on-screen, who were clearly trying to teach us A Lesson.

"If you think you can get away with bickering, immature antics when the weight of an entire world rests on your shoulders—think again," Dr. Takumi says, his voice a steely threat. "Don't forget who actually controls this ship. You are merely its custodians. This means following our instructions, agree with them or not. Do you copy?"

"Y-yes, sir."

I mouth the words along with my teammates, but inside I am seething. I knew Dr. Takumi was made of ice, but he at least used to put on a better show. If this is how he's exerting his influence on day one, I don't even want to think about what he'll be up to by the time we get to Mars.

"All right, team," Beckett says, jumping into his "leader" role early. "Let's move on to the rest of the tour."

No one dares contradict him while Takumi and Sokolov are still watching, but I can feel our collective resentment as we fall into step behind Beckett. The Final Six have been in space for less than an hour, but the hostility is heating up already.

THREE

I THOUGHT GRETA SHOWED ME EVERYTHING WHEN SHE GAVE me the grand tour of Wagner Enterprises two days ago, but it turns out she was holding back the most important part. She leads me there now, through hallways that seem to go on forever and hidden doors that appear like a magic trick behind cabinets and bookshelves, until we reach a tiny elevator at the end of the third floor. It's so small that I have to hunch over to fit inside with Greta, and I have a feeling it was designed that way on purpose—to keep people out.

She swipes her keycard against the button marked with a *U*, and the elevator swoops four floors down, dropping us off in a windowless corridor underground. Looming straight ahead is an armed guard standing in front of two heavy steel doors. I swallow hard, suddenly uneasy about what I might find.

"The lab you saw before is indeed the official Wagner Enterprises facility, but *this* is where I keep my most high-security work," Greta says, striding toward the doors. "I call it my bulletproof lair of secrets." She nods at the guard. "Afternoon, Nikolas."

"Afternoon, ma'am."

He opens the door, and we step through the threshold. At first all I see is a blank white foyer, empty except for an open cabinet with uniforms tucked inside. Greta hands me a white lab coat and a clear helmet she calls a "bionic face shield," and then, once we've both donned our gear, she leads me around the corner—where the wall falls away, and the view begins.

We're standing at a railing looking down, deeper underground, at a sprawling space as big as the ISTC Mission Floor. Towering clear shelves display what seem to be thousands of foreign-looking specimens, and a long lab table stretches half the width of the room, occupied by just three scientists studying samples under microscopes. They must be the lucky few Greta trusts in here, and I can't help thinking about what Naomi would give to be one of them. It seems . . . wrong almost, that I'm the one exploring her hero's domain. But maybe—if I'm lucky—it can be the first thing I tell her about when we meet again.

"This way." Greta motions me forward and I follow her down the stairs and onto the lab floor, past the microscope tables and conveyor belts of robotic machinery, until we reach a black curtain. There's another heavy steel door behind it, and before entering, Greta reaches her palm up to the wall. My eyes widen as a rectangular portion of the wall edges forward at her touch, jutting out like an opened drawer. It's some kind of . . . camouflaged locker?

Greta turns an unseen knob and the cabinet in the wall swings open. I peer over her shoulder, but before I can identify anything among the shadowy heap of items, she pulls out two heavy-looking down coats and seals the locker shut. I watch in confusion as Greta slips hers on over her lab uniform and hands me the other. Of all the things I expected her to grab from this secret stash, another *coat* wasn't one of them. But once we step through this new door, I feel the chill, my teeth beginning to chatter.

"Welcome to 'Europa,'" Greta says, the lights switching on automatically at a flick of her wrist.

My eyes widen as the room transforms from dark shadows to . . . a miniature world of ice. A thick frozen shell lined with blood-red ridges and cracks stretches beneath my feet and around the lab, covering the length of a stadium. I take a step forward and yelp as my body bounces up in the air. I land with a thud halfway across the ice, laughing in astonishment.

"How did you do this?"

"It's just a climate-controlled vacuum chamber with the floors engineered to mimic Europa's lower gravity," she answers breezily. "It was crucial for me to re-create a portion of the environment in order to test and study what kind of life could form and survive on the real Europa. Watch out behind you, by the way."

I turn around and then scramble forward with another, clumsier flying leap. There's a field of lethal-looking frozen *spikes* behind me, their blades more than three times my height.

"What are those things?"

"They're penitentes. Spires of ice and snow," Greta explains, looking at them as though they're something to be admired as much as feared. "They're caused by sublimation on the surface, so there's no getting rid of them, at least not until Europa is terraformed. Right now, penitentes have only been confirmed at the equator, so Dr. Takumi and General Sokolov have the *Pontus* landing at Thera Macula, the chaos terrain, instead. Which is one of the reasons why the Final Six need our intervention." Her eyes take on a new intensity as she looks at me. "Navigating your way around giant ice spikes is nothing compared to what is likely waiting at Thera Macula."

My heart starts beating faster.

"What do you mean?"

"The ISTC was right to set their sights on Europa," she says, her foot tracing one of the red grooves of the model moon. "It is a world made for life. But they missed the most important discovery of all. . . . Follow me."

Adjacent to the mock-up of Europa's surface is an arcade-like stall, a compact structure that reminds me of the old-fashioned shooting games at Oasi Park back in Rome. I find a strange-looking gun holstered to the railing when we step inside, with a target straight ahead—but instead of a wall of candy-colored prizes, the target is just a huge chunk of ice, floating behind a barbed-wire fence. *What in the world?*

"Popular science tells us that these red lines crisscrossing the surface are nothing more than the effects of radiation-blasted sea salt flowing upward from Europa's buried ocean. But I always had another suspicion," she begins. "During my time under contract with ISTC, while designing the *Pontus*, I found an opportunity to test my hypothesis: by mimicking the conditions of Europa right here, inside this vacuum chamber. I took a sample of the sodium chloride that was retrieved from the earlier robotic mission, combined it with water, and froze it to the same temperature you will find on Europa's surface."

I watch, still not quite following her, as Greta pulls the rocket-shaped gun out of its holster.

"And now, through this tool, we can re-create the effect of years' worth of radiation."

Greta fires the gun, and I'm transfixed as electron beams start flying through the air, leaving glowing blue lines in their wake when they hit the salted ice. After several strikes, she beckons me forward for a closer look.

I raise my eyebrows. The electron rays did make an impact—but instead of Europa's defining dark lines, they show up as light-colored circles dotting the ice. So . . . what does it mean?

"I spent hours, days, *months* testing this," Greta tells me. "A few hours of direct, up-close radiation blasting is equivalent to a hundred or so years of what Europa experiences on the surface, yet none of the effects I found here came close to resembling the red ridges. So I tried something else."

She leads me out of the stall, back to the model Europa. This time, she instructs me to place my hand on one of the crisscrossing ridges—and I jump as the lines light up, vibrations and heat fizzing under my palm.

"What was that?"

"I re-created the placement of the anomalous signatures that the robots, Cyb and Dot, picked up through their magnetometers when probing Europa's magnetic field," she says, her tone as matter-of-fact as if "re-creating anomalous signatures" is some kind of everyday activity. I'm still trying to figure out what half those words even mean when she continues, "Notice where the strongest energy is felt: the same surface coordinates where—as your friend Naomi already uncovered—the biosignatures of chlorophyll and methane were found. The darkest division of red ridges."

She takes a breath, looking at me with eyes more animated than I've seen them yet.

"The signatures build and increase when you follow the lines in a specific pattern—one I've spent more than a year deciphering. Do you realize what this means?"

"Um. Maybe? You do know I wasn't drafted to space camp for my science abilities, right?" I manage a grin, even as I feel a pang in my chest for Naomi. If only she were here—then this might all make sense.

"Europa's red ridges, the veins of this moon, make up a *map*!" The words come tumbling out of her, a note of triumph in her voice. "It's a map that shows us where Europa's ancient alien life once existed, but is no more—and where its current life thrives. On Thera Macula." She draws in a breath. "Only I know how to read it. And with my help, *you* will be able to swim its route, and lead the others to the clear Habitable Zone."

I can feel the blood roaring in my ears as I stare at her.

"If this is real, then why—why haven't you told everyone? Why aren't the space agencies and ISTC working on it, showing the Final Six how to navigate the map right now?"

"Of course I told them," she says curtly. "But they refused to hear me, because accepting the map as reality would require them to publicly acknowledge the existence of extraterrestrial life on Europa—that it's not ours for the taking. And that's something the mission leaders will never do. They've risen to unforeseen power and prominence based on this dream they've sold to the world, and my findings threaten that dream. Our disagreement on this point is what ended our work together. So now I bring the question to you."

She looks in my eyes, her steely-blue gaze so intent it makes me flinch.

"Do you believe? Are you willing to risk it all, to face

down potential terrors more frightening than death, for my hypothesis? For the chance that we might actually salvage this mission?"

And for Naomi.

"I'll do it." My hands shake, but my voice remains steady. "I understand what I'm signing up for . . . and I'll take my chances."

FOUR

NAOMI

MOMENTS AFTER DR. TAKUMI AND GENERAL SOKOLOV SIGN off, their images on-screen fizzling to static, the hatch door to the Astronauts' Residence swings open. I freeze, half convinced one of them is about to walk through the hatch in another "gotcha!" moment. But then I hear the whir of machinery and the precise, mechanical footsteps that could only belong to something nonhuman. Sure enough, it's our new backup robot, Tera—the AI who is only here because of my mistake.

My stomach twists as I look up at Tera's bronze mask of a face, at the electronic suit of armor that makes up her body. *You were supposed to be Dot.* If it wasn't for me hacking into the AI back at space camp, tricking Dot into retrieving and showing me the classified Europa data, then Tera would still be in Houston, undergoing new model testing, while Dot—the safer, proven robot—would be the one sharing the ship with us. But instead, because of me, she is an empty vessel back on Earth with her memory and settings scrubbed, while Tera was rushed through production ahead of schedule to make our launch. I try to swallow the guilt as I glance from the unfamiliar robot to my crewmates, and back again. I can only hope my mistake won't cost us much more.

The robots are humanoids, meaning their design is loosely based on our bodies: between six and seven feet tall, with two legs and two arms, ten fingers, but no toes. Sensors and encoders fill the gaps where organs should be, while the Artificial Intelligence Operating System (AIOS), the brains and heart that make the robots tick, is held within a touch screen hidden behind the metal plates of their torsos.

"Hello, astronauts," Tera greets us in a soft voice that strikes me as a beat too slow. "I'm here to show you around the rest of your quarters."

Chaperoned again. What was even the *point* of Dr. Takumi and the general giving Beckett this false sense of power over us when they clearly don't intend on ever leaving us alone? I guess it's a contingency plan, but still—him? Nothing adds up.

I follow Tera and my crewmates into the elevator pod, which feels like a flying jump as it ascends to the next floor. Here, on the left side of the atrium, we find a gym with cardio machines, stationary bikes, and weights, while something called "SpaceTube Fitness" plays on the overhead screen: a guided workout starring an annoyingly perky, high-ponytailed athlete who beams into the camera through her sprints. Something tells me I won't look quite so peppy when it's my turn.

"To prevent bone loss in space, and to remain at optimal health for the duration of our trip, you will each be assigned ninety minutes of fitness, five days per week," Tera says in the monotone drawl of someone reciting preprogrammed words. I groan aloud at that one. Tera's head swivels in my direction, registering my reaction.

"It isn't so bad. Each machine connects to the above virtual reality screen. You can select scenes to accompany your workouts, such as running through a forest while on the treadmill, or boating through the Pacific while using the rowing machine."

"You mean—it'll feel like we're back on Earth?" Sydney's voice rises with hope, and I feel a rush of warmth toward her. Maybe I'm not the only one who wasn't so ready to leave.

"Correct," Tera answers. "Though you will also find a few scenes set on Europa. Moving along . . ."

She leads us around the curve to the other wing of the second floor. The smell of disinfectant greets us first, and my heart sinks as soon as I see the exam table and the white cabinet marked *Devices—Sterile*. We're in the medical bay. I'd almost managed to put out of my mind what happens here.

"Your evenings will follow the same routine as at space camp, beginning here at six p.m. with an injection of radiation-resistant bacteria, followed by dinner upstairs. Sydney, as mission medical officer, you will administer and supervise the injections."

"Roger that," she says while my stomach plummets and my palms begin to sweat. *We can't—we can't let it in again.* Not after losing Callum and Suki, not after I learned the truth about the serum. There has to be another way for us to stave off the radiation on Europa without injecting *alien cells* into our bodies. We already have a next-gen heat shield protecting us through our space suits, so maybe I could spend my time on the ship designing something else wearable instead of us taking this risk—

"Naomi?"

Jian's voice pulls me back to the moment, where I see my crewmates filing into the elevator pod behind Tera. I force my thoughts away from the RRB conundrum—if only for now—and fall into step with the rest.

The third floor is the kitchen and dining area, with one section for food prep and storage, the other for bolted-down seating. Four smaller round-top tables surround the main dining table for six, thankfully giving us a choice between eating as a group or on our own. It's already asking a *lot* for us near-strangers to spend the rest of our lives together without losing all sanity. I'm pretty sure if that included sitting for a mandatory three meals a day together too, some fork stabbings would inevitably follow.

"General Sokolov has mandated that you will take turns preparing meals for the group. We'll go in alphabetical order, beginning tonight with Naomi Ardalan. And now, one floor up, you'll find your bed-and-baths."

We quicken our footsteps, all of us eager to see the one place we can claim as ours alone, free from the cameras and observing eyes. Upstairs, we find six identical capsules with sliding teak doors, three on each side of the atrium.

"Boys on the left, girls to the right," Tera directs us. "Your bags have been brought up from the cargo module, and are waiting in your respective rooms."

My heart ticks a beat faster at the thought of getting to see *my stuff* again. It's only been a day since I packed, but the physical distance makes it seem so much longer—like I haven't laid eyes on my clothes or books or photographs in months.

There are no names posted to the doors, but when Tera taps the mini-tablet screen attached to her bronze wrist, they slide open on cue, revealing a row of matching interiors distinguished only by the bags sitting on the beds. As soon as I spot my two navy blue duffels from home, I run forward, into the 120-square-foot compartment serving as my bedroom.

I know we're lucky to even have individual rooms, considering the astronauts before us had to make do with shared bunk beds, but still—this is *tiny*. The bed takes up the vast majority, with a few rows of shelving built into the wall beside it. There's no real floor space, unless you count the few steps between the bed and the plexiglass-enclosed "bathroom" behind it: basically a toilet, shower, and sink all within tripping distance of each other. But there's a porthole window above my pillow, and I lie on my stomach to peer out of it now. I can see the stars, the same wash of glitter against black that I used to look up at from Earth. The sight makes me feel just a little bit calmer, a little more at home.

I sit up on the bed, opening one of my duffels and riffling inside. We had to remove all jewelry for liftoff, and there are two pieces I'm looking for now that I need to hold against my skin. The first is Leo's signet ring, with its swooping, carved cursive *D* for Danieli. The second is my grandmother's necklace from Iran, which was passed down to me on my fifteenth birthday: a delicate gold chain with a large teardrop-shaped turquoise stone. With the ring on my finger and the turquoise around my neck, I feel like myself again . . . and that feeling makes it easier to stop feeling sorry for myself, to remember that I'm not just a passive player here. Maybe I never wanted to be drafted, but as the finalist who found out the truth—or at least half the truth—about Europa's hidden extraterrestrial life, I need to be here. There's no one else to solve the mystery of what's waiting for us, or how to survive it.

I pull a notepad and pen out of my bag, forced to go low-tech after my flash drive was erased the same morning Dot was reset. But the ISTC couldn't scrub my memory. I start jotting down everything I remember of the data I scooped from Dot, hoping that if I can see it all written in a row—the DNA properties, chemical elements, and cell types—I can form a picture from the clues.

I don't realize I've fallen asleep until my earpiece starts chirping with a robotic voice. "Good evening, Naomi. You are expected in the medical bay in exactly twenty minutes. Please meet your crew there."

I roll over with a groan, punching my pillow in frustration. Clearly I'm not going to come up with a way out of the RRB injection in just twenty minutes. I have no choice but to face the needle—and hope I won't be the next one to have a reaction.

Something is crinkling under my hip, and I scoot over, rescuing my notes from getting wrinkled beyond recognition. I glance at the page, covered with scribbled words, formulas, and numbers that don't reveal any pattern just yet. But I know from experience that it can sometimes take reading the same data fifty times before an answer or conclusion jumps out at you.

I drag myself off the bed and out of my room, stepping into the elevator pod at the same time as Jian. We smile hello, but there's a nervous energy in the pod as we swoop down to the second floor. I wonder if Jian is as leery of the RRB as I am. And then an old exchange between us comes flashing back to my mind.

"Last night, when Suki was having her—her reaction to the RRB, she kept repeating something in Mandarin. . . . It sounded like 'tā hái huózhe.' Is that—is that a real phrase?"

I'll never forget the way he stared at me then.

"She was saying, 'It's alive.'"

I watch him now, his brow furrowed in thought. Is he remembering the same thing? But before I can ask, the elevator spits us out on the second floor, where Minka, Dev, and Beckett are already gathered.

My stomach flip-flops with every step we take to the medical bay and the waiting chair. Suki's face floods my mind—my roommate and friend, transformed into a clawing, screaming stranger the night after her third dose. I think of Callum, of his kind blue eyes, shut forever that same week. They said it wouldn't happen to us, that we'd know by now if we were in the small percentage to experience side effects. But that was back on Earth. No one had tested the serum for an extended period of time in space before. What if that changes our reactions? *What if I'm next?*

Sydney is waiting for us, wearing a white medic's coat over an ivory sweater and black pants, her hair pulled back in a ponytail that highlights her beautiful dark brown skin and hazel eyes. The medical uniform helps her slip into the role, serious and professional as she swirls the viscous blue serum into a syringe, then plunges the needle without blinking. I'm not surprised to find Tera is back, standing watch, with her camera-eyes beaming down to Earth proof of the Final Six following protocols.

I hang back, waiting to go last and willing something to happen that could distract from my turn. But all too soon, I'm the only one left, and everyone's looking my way, waiting for me to get this over with so I can get to the kitchen and prep our first meal. My throat is like sandpaper as I walk to Sydney's chair and pull up my sleeve. The pain fires up my arm as she presses down on the needle, and then my hands fly to my head as an image enters, unbidden.

Dark water is climbing like a chimney, oozing a smoky substance, emitting a low, vibrational hum. I try to move away from it, but something slithers against my skin, and I stop cold—

"Naomi! You okay?"

My eyes snap open. Whatever I just saw—thought I saw—is gone. It's only Sydney, looking down at me in concern while the rest of our team mills about, oblivious to my second of madness.

"Yeah," I mutter, my face flushing. "I just—thought I saw something . . . weird."

But when Sydney bends down to apply the bandage, I make a split-second decision.

"I have something to tell you. Tonight, after dinner."

FIVE

LEO

SOMEONE IS PLAYING PIANO IN A PLACE WHERE MUSIC
doesn't belong. I've never heard anyone play like this
before—like there's a fever in their hands and the only cure
can be found in the keys. It's a melody of rolling minor
notes, the kind that tugs at your chest and pulls out whatever
might be hiding there. I see my parents and sister, jumping
up and down in time with the music as they wave Italian
flags outside the *WagnerOne* rocket launch site. My face
hurts from smiling, it's so good to see them again—*alive*
again. And then, a blink later, Naomi is floating in front of
me, her dark hair falling like a cloud in front of her face as
she leans forward to whisper something in my ear. I grin in
response, taking her hand to spin her around—but I must

have been too fast, too clumsy, because now she's looking down at her finger in panic. *"The ring!"*

It's gone. The signet ring I gave her has slipped off, floating away into the void. I lunge forward to catch it, but now I'm the one falling, away from her. The music seems all wrong suddenly as it continues to play, too upbeat, too loud—

I sit up in bed with a gasp. *Just a dream.* It was just an anxiety dream, to be expected when—as Greta keeps reminding me—I'm about to take the most daunting spaceflight in history. Except . . . I still hear the music. It couldn't be more out of place in this austere, left-brain environment, but there it is.

My eyes dart up to the guest room's coffered ceiling. It sounds like the piano is coming from there, upstairs in Greta's suite. And now I'm even more intrigued. It's almost impossible to imagine this melody, this soul, pouring out of a mind so consumed with numbers, formulas, and facts. What else does she have up her sleeve?

I imagine what Naomi would say if I told her I discovered a whole new side to her idol, a secret talent no one knows about. I can bring her the story like a gift. It just requires a little effort.

I hoist myself out of bed, throwing on a T-shirt and sweats over my boxers before moving to the door. I've spent the least amount of time here in the domestic wing, so I don't really know my way around—but I do remember seeing a staircase at the end of the hall.

I make my way through the dark, the blinking lights of all the wireless tech giving off just enough of a glow to guide my steps. The stone staircase is cold beneath my bare feet, and I jog the last few stairs to a carpeted wing, where Greta lives. It's my first time seeing this section of the compound, and even through the dark, I can tell that it's impressive.

I track the piano's rising volume, passing a series of doors until I reach the one that is slightly ajar. It looks like some sort of private library, with floor-to-ceiling bookshelves, a touch-screen desk, a leather couch and armchair, and there in the corner, a baby grand. But—the piano bench is empty. The keys are moving on their own, programmed to impress, just like everything else in this place.

The crush of disappointment catches me by surprise. It shouldn't matter that the "musician" who moved me to leave my room in the middle of the night turned out to be fake, but it does. Maybe some part of me needed to believe that the person taking my life in her hands, sending me to space on my own—had that kind of soul.

Instead, Greta is standing behind her desk, studying and swiping at the touch screen as if it's the middle of a workday instead of two in the morning. On the opposite wall, right above the piano, a flat-screen monitor flashes with images and symbols I haven't seen before. They move too fast for me to register what they are, exactly, except for one: a double helix, the structure of DNA. We spent a whole school year on this topic, back in my former life. And then I notice what might be the strangest sight yet. The images on the monitor are moving in tandem with the notes to the song.

Greta lifts her head, and that's when I see her lips moving—mouthing something intently while staring at the screen. I squint, trying to decipher what she's saying. Is it the letter *B* or *D*? I'm almost sure I can make out the word "minor." And then the hairs on the back of my neck stand up.

It's like she's conducting an invisible player with just her voice, reading the sheet music aloud, while each note in the song corresponds with an image on-screen: a block of numbers, a string of DNA—and *my face.*

My heart jumps in my throat. I squeeze my eyes shut and open them again, but when the minor chord progression returns, so does my photograph. It's the same dated photo that circulated in the media when I was first drafted to ISTC.

The screen freezes on my face; the piano stops. And then a new, spare melody fills the room, coming from somewhere else—a response. That's when the screen floods with a row of foreign symbols, washing across my photo. Greta's lips curve upward in a smile, and I feel a trickle of fear. Who is she having this coded, clandestine conversation with about me? And . . . what does it mean?

Greta's head turns sharply and I scramble back against the wall, holding my breath. *She heard me.*

I inch my way along the wall in the opposite direction,

biting my lip to keep from making a sound. After a few moments of Greta eyeing the dark outside her door, she finally turns back to the screens, and I take off in a silent run down the corridor. I come to a halt at the end of the hallway, in front of a door that's halfway open. There's no staircase on this side of the corridor, so I'm stuck here until Greta closes her door and I can get by her unseen. I might as well hide out in this empty-looking room until the coast is clear.

I take a tentative step inside. My eyes adjust to the darkness, and I let out an exhale of relief at the ordinary sight in front of me: empty bed, desk, dresser, and TV console. Must be another guest room. I flick on the light.

Something cold grips my chest. All it takes is one look for me to know I'm standing in the room of someone who doesn't live here anymore—who wasn't planning to leave.

The room is like a time capsule from five years ago. There's an old calendar hanging on the wall, sharing space with posters of Europop bands I remember being big back then. The bed isn't just empty, it's unmade and gathering dust with a half-open backpack tossed at the foot of it. The desk is littered with school papers written in German, and I can clearly make out the date scrawled across the top. I spot a corkboard of photos above the desk, and I stop in my tracks.

The boy in all the photos looks the same age as me, and bears a striking resemblance to Greta. The similarities are right there on display in the one picture of the two of them together, smiling almost identical smiles at the top of a ski slope.

She had a son. What happened to him?

Since I arrived here, there hasn't been a single sign of Greta having a family, not now or in the past. And the idea of a Greta 2.0 the same age as me and Naomi is the kind of info I know she would have relished and told me about, so it must not be public knowledge. But why keep her son a secret?

I glance around the eerily preserved bedroom one last time before bolting out of there, nearly tripping over my own feet in my haste to get away.

I thought Greta was my lifeline, handing me the answer to my prayers. But now, for the first time since her plane picked me up from Johnson Space Center—I wonder if I was right to say yes to her.

"Morning, Mr. Danieli! It's time to begin today's training. Dr. Wagner is waiting for you in the lab."

I unearth my head from under the pillow and find myself looking sideways at a silver, compact humanoid robot wheeling up to my bed with a tray. It's Greta's butler, Corion.

Greta. For a second I can't remember why I feel a prickly, unsettled sensation at her name, and then the memory of last night comes flooding back. After I snuck back down to my room, I used the guest tablet to dig for answers online, but anything I tried—"Dr. Greta Wagner son," "Dr. Wagner child," or any variation of the words—returned zero results. It's the only time I've ever seen that happen, as if those search terms were blocked . . . or something.

I slump against the pillows, wanting to just stay here and avoid facing Greta and all her secrets. But then, giving up on her would mean losing my one ticket to Europa. To Naomi.

"Are you all right, Mr. Danieli?"

Corion's eyes swivel outward, peering closer at me, as he sets down a tray with coffee and breakfast at the foot of the bed.

"Y-yeah. Just groggy. And you can call me Leo."

Mr. Danieli will always be my father to me, no matter how long he's been gone.

"Copy that, Leo. I'll wait outside for you to eat and dress, and then I'll escort you to meet Dr. Wagner." He pulls open the dresser drawer that used to be empty, now suddenly full of folded shirts and pants. "We noticed you didn't arrive with much in the way of clothing, so Dr. Wagner instructed me to bring you these. They should all be in your size."

"Th-thanks."

My mind flashes to the guy in the photograph from the abandoned bedroom—my age, my size. A pit forms in my stomach at the thought of wearing his clothes, and I cross my fingers that I'm wrong, that I'll find brand-new clothing instead. But when Corion leaves and I glance in the drawer, none of the clothes have any tags. They could easily be his. And there's no way to explain my reluctance to wear them without revealing last night's snooping.

I take a deep breath and slip one of the shirts over my

head, trying to ignore the creepy feeling crawling up my spine. I step into a pair of track pants and my own sneakers, and then hurry out the door, where Corion is waiting. He briefs me on the day ahead while we make our way to the underground lab.

"You will begin on the flight simulator, practicing liftoff from Earth. From there, you'll move into a run-through of the critical Mars maneuver."

"Right." I nod, trying to appear more confident than I feel. The Mars intercept is the single trickiest task of this whole solo mission. I can't afford even the smallest mistake, if I have any prayer of docking with the Final Six.

At the opposite end of the lab from the Europa surface mock-up, Corion shows me to the replica *WagnerOne* rocket, wired with the training sim software. Greta is waiting for me outside, leaning against the machinery with her head bent over her tablet screen. The sight of her silver hair and pale, creased skin gives me a jolt of nerves after last night. Am I crazy to still trust her blindly, without asking about what I saw? Then again, I can't picture her taking kindly to being spied on. I have to swallow my questions and form my own conclusions. And right now, my conclusion is that she's all I've got.

I hold my breath as her ice-blue eyes fix on me. Her stoic mask slips for a second, so brief that I would have missed it if I hadn't known to look. But it's there, something like hope in her eyes, at the sight of me in these borrowed clothes. I drop my gaze to the floor.

"Morning, Leo," she says after a beat. "Are you ready to learn how this ship flies?"

"Yes, ma'am."

"Good. Now, I understand the ISTC focused your training on underwater specialties, and didn't provide you much in the way of flight training," she begins. "So while I'm busy tending to other areas of your launch, I've brought on someone whose round-the-clock focus can be preparing you for piloting your own craft. At the same time, you'll receive a crash course on surviving space travel from an experienced former astronaut."

"Okay. This sounds promising." I feel my spirits lift. Greta can't be *too* unstable if she's going to all this effort to make sure I'm safe. What I saw last night in her study must have just been the eccentric-genius version of preparing a mission. And as for her family secret . . . well, it's none of my business, is it?

"All right, you two," Greta calls into the training capsule behind her. "Come on out!"

The hatch door opens. And when I see them step outside, I could swear I'm dreaming.

"*Asher?!*" I run to my friend, throwing my arms around him. "And *Lark*!" I pull her into our hug, and for a moment it's like we're kids again, jumping and hugging and yelling our excitement. I pull back, an arm slung around each of their shoulders, drinking in the sight of their faces. "I can't believe you're both here!"

"Same." Asher grins. "It's great to see you, man."

"How did this happen?" I stare at the two of them in amazement. "How'd you get this past Dr. Takumi and the general?"

Lark grimaces. "Um. I basically had to jump ship."

"Lark is our newest hire at Wagner Enterprises," Greta says with a proud smile. "And her first decision as mission strategist was to bring in Asher for your flight training."

I beam at Lark.

"That was a great decision, all right. But what happened with you and the ISTC? You seemed so committed to Dr. Takumi and the mission."

I knew Lark was enough of a rebel to orchestrate the flight switch when I was supposed to get shipped back to Italy, by sending in Greta's disguised jet in place of the official Italy plane. But I never would have predicted her leaving ISTC and NASA altogether.

Lark lets out a long exhale.

"It was a long time coming, really. I mean, I did believe in the mission at first, and for a long time I saw my career path as following in the general's footsteps. But then I started to sense something shady was underfoot with the two of them, especially after what happened on the *Athena*." She looks away. "Do you know the name Remi Anders?"

"Yes."

Remi was one of the astronauts on the doomed mission to Mars five years ago. The failure of that mission and the tragedy of losing their entire crew is what led to a complete reorganization of NASA, with Dr. Takumi replacing the previous leader, and partnering with General Sokolov and the other international space agencies to develop a new, airtight Plan B. But even though so much has changed since *Athena*, and we're going to an entirely different place in the solar system, that never stopped Naomi from worrying about history repeating itself.

"Well . . . Remi was my fiancé."

"Oh." My breath catches. "I—I'm sorry."

You would think that with all the death I've seen, it would make it easier for me to talk about. But I still never have the right words.

"Thanks," she mumbles. "Anyway. I know they concluded the astronauts all died, but without any bodies or concrete proof, I always wondered if he might still be out there somewhere. That was one of my main reasons for staying with the ISTC—to see if the closer I got to Dr. Takumi, the more answers I'd find."

"Did—did it work?" I ask.

She shakes her head bitterly. "I wish. And then, once I saw what happened to Suki and Callum at training camp, I knew the Final Six weren't safe." She looks up defiantly. "I had to do something to help—before the Europa Mission turns out like Mars."

The thought gives me a chill. So she thinks the same as Naomi.

"Lark proved her ingenuity when she reached out to me

the day after the Final Six selections were made," Greta speaks up. "She was the first—and so far the only—person to figure out that I'm the mind behind the Space Conspirator."

Asher's head jerks up.

"What? You are?"

I meet his eyes and nod. Naomi was the first one to tell me about the Space Conspirator—the anonymous science blog that went viral after the *Athena* disaster, when everyone was looking for answers to what happened. Even I, a thirteen-year-old kid in Italy at the time with no connection to NASA, can remember family conversations around the table at Sunday lunch, with all of us theorizing what went wrong for the doomed astronauts. Nowadays, Naomi says the website's focus is on proving that life exists on Europa and beyond, that we're not alone. I guess that's where I come in.

"How did you figure out it was Greta?" I ask Lark, suddenly remembering that Naomi doesn't know. I can't wait to see the look on her face when I tell her—

"It was in the coding," Lark says with a modest shrug. "There was a shorthand in the IP algorithm that reminded me of something similar I'd seen in the *Pontus* software, which I knew Greta programmed."

"Ah." I nod, even though that just went over my head.

"After she figured me out, Lark said she knew I was up to a countermission and wanted to help." Greta gestures to me. "And you know the rest."

"Ash, what about you?" I ask, still incredulous that my

old space camp roommate and buddy is here. "Does your brother know where you are?"

"Yeah, but I swore him to secrecy. I think he was as excited as I was when we heard from Lark," he says with a chuckle. "I mean . . . I wasn't the same when I came home after eliminations. I wanted it so bad, and to be so close and then get cut—" He breaks off midsentence. "Well, I know you know how that feels."

"And now you've come all this way to help me go to Europa," I say with a pang of guilt. "That must seem unfair, especially when you're the one who actually knows how to fly a spacecraft. . . ." My voice trails off.

"It's okay," he says, and I can tell he means it. "The ship basically runs by itself, aside from liftoff and docking—the two main things I'll be training you in. It's the other stuff, the dealing with unknowns underwater, that no one can really teach, but you can actually *do*. So it should be you. It should have been you from the start, instead of that obnoxious Beckett Wolfe."

"Thanks," I tell him. "You might be an even better friend than I deserve."

"And now it's time we got on with said training," Greta says, glancing down at her wrist monitor. "It won't be long before Dr. Takumi finds out that Leo never made it to Italy, and that Lark and Asher are missing too. Chances are, he'll put two and two together and end up here. We need to get Leo launched, and the two of you out of here, before he does."

My chest tightens. I've put my friends at risk, and who knows what will happen to them once I'm off in space, unable to help them the way they've helped me? But when I look back at the two of them, I don't see fear or doubt. They look proud, determined. And I'm so grateful, I can't speak.

SIX

NAOMI

WE SIT AROUND THE TABLE EYEING EACH OTHER AS REALITY sinks in. There's no Cyb or Tera here to break the tension, no Dr. Takumi or General Sokolov on-screen to distract us. We don't even have a video screen in the dining room to connect us with the outside world, though the blinking red lights of the cameras are omnipresent as ever.

It's just the six of us, alone in the universe.

Sydney is the first to break the silence. "It's so quiet up here. Too quiet. Does anyone want some music or something?"

"What kind of music?" Beckett asks skeptically while the rest of us immediately say yes, grasping at anything to make this night a little more bearable.

Sydney glances up at the ceiling, wired with sensors built to listen to and follow our commands. "Dinner Music playlist."

A hypnotic mid-tempo track starts playing, the singer's breathy vocals like silk against an electro beat. The background music makes it easier for us to talk, and Dev asks, "Why do you guys think we were the ones chosen?"

When no one answers, he laughs. "Isn't this the part where we all brag about ourselves?"

"I think it's obvious enough," Jian says with a shrug. "It was just based on our skills and the roles the mission leaders needed to fill. I must have been the best pilot of the bunch, just like Sydney was at the top when it came to medicine and biology, and so on."

"Sure. But we were all up against stiff competition for our roles here," Dev reminds him. "Isn't it hard to say who was really better at what? I think there had to have been more to the decision. Our winning personalities, maybe?" He wiggles his eyebrows at Sydney, and she gives him a playful shove. Watching them, I'm reminded that they were on the same training team. They're probably close, and relieved to have each other here. I push my plate away, my stomach suddenly hurting.

"I think they knew exactly who they wanted from the beginning," Beckett says, stretching his arms behind his head with his usual arrogant air. "Our time at space camp only confirmed it."

He meets my eyes, his pointed look daring me to

contradict him. But even though I know he didn't get here honestly, that he manipulated himself onto the team and Leo out of it, I don't say anything. *Yet.*

"What was the president talking to you about on Air Force One?" I ask instead, with all the faux-civility I can muster. "You seemed to be awfully deep in conversation."

"I was saying good-bye to my *uncle*," Beckett says, as if anyone could forget their relation. "That's it."

He's lying. There was more to that conversation. I could feel it when I watched it take place—and I wonder if it's the reason for Beckett's sudden boost in status on the ship.

"What I want to know is how two Americans ended up on this mission," Minka says, looking from me to Beckett with an unfriendly gaze. "I thought it was supposed to be an international effort, but instead, we have *three* from primarily English-speaking countries?" She turns her glance on Sydney. "It seems NASA received preferential treatment, and none for Roscosmos or ESA."

"Uh, Canada has our own space agency, remember?" Sydney retorts. "You don't need to lump me in with NASA."

"And it was supposed to be just one American," I add under my breath.

Beckett turns his glowering stare on me.

"What did you say?"

I raise my chin, meeting his eyes.

"I said it would have been just one American, if they'd chosen the underwater specialist who always came first in our training. Leo Danieli."

Beckett shoves his chair back from the table, anger twisting his face into something ugly.

"Take that back," he hisses. "You better apologize before I come up with a punishment for you. Did you already forget who's in charge when Takumi and Sokolov aren't around?"

"Guys, guys." Jian holds up his hands. "Calm down. No one is punishing anyone. It's our first night here, we're all away from home and going through something no one prepares you for—it's only natural for there to be some tension. Let's just . . . let it go."

"He's right," Sydney says. "C'mon, Beckett. Sit down."

For a minute I think he's going to blow up at her, too. But then he drops back into his seat with a huff, shooting me a warning glare. I'm not looking at him, though.

I'm watching as Dev and Sydney exchange a glance—a look I must have shared a hundred times with Leo when we were at space camp. The kind of glance that manages to say, *How did we end up with these train wrecks and all their drama?* and, at the same time, *Thank God you're here.*

And looking at them now, I've never felt more alone.

Between 11:00 p.m. and 7:00 a.m. UTC (Coordinated Universal Time), the *Pontus* goes into Power-Conservation Mode, shutting down the lights and any nonessential equipment and electronics. The six of us retreat to our rooms an hour before then, attempting to settle in for our first night's sleep in the most surreal of surroundings. But instead of getting into bed, I wait for the darkness to fall, and for the cameras to switch off with the lights. And then I slip out the door, feeling my way along the walls to the next compartment.

I give Sydney's door a light tap and she appears right away, wearing cozy blue pajamas with her black curls piled up in a messy bun. She motions me inside, where there's barely enough floor space for both of us, and then perches at the foot of the bed with a flashlight, which bathes the room in an eerie glow.

"So what did you want to talk to me about?"

She pats the comforter next to her, and as I sit down, my mind scrambles for the best way to begin. Part of me thinks I might be crazy to share all this with someone I barely know, but Sydney is the one injecting the alien bacteria into all of us. If there's a single person on this ship who needs to hear the truth, it's her.

"Um. You know how Dev was asking why we think we each got chosen?" I start. "Well, in my case, it's because of what I know—what I found out." I raise my eyes to hers. "I'm the one who hacked Dot."

"What?" Sydney's jaw drops. "Are you kidding?"

"'Fraid not."

"How could you—*why* would you—do that?"

"Because we'd just lost Suki and Callum, and I knew it had to do with the RRB and Europa," I say, my voice coming out more defensive than I intended. I take a deep breath.

"I could tell there was a lot that Dr. Takumi and the general were hiding, so I took matters into my own hands. I just didn't think I'd get caught, or that anything would happen to Dot. . . ." My voice trails off in guilt, and I can't help noticing how Sydney shifts away from me, closer to the edge of the bed.

"And you're saying Dr. Takumi drafted you to keep you quiet about whatever this—this *intel* is?" Sydney gives me a suspicious look, clearly doubting my story.

"That, and the fact that I accidentally proved to him I'm the one for the job," I say wryly. "Dr. Takumi knew that anyone who could hack into their high-security robotics system would be able to handle the tech on the ship."

"Okay . . . Go on."

"Before I tell you what I found out, will you promise to just keep an open mind, and also keep it between us?" I ask her. "What I'm about to say might sound far-fetched, but it's all true and vetted."

Sydney looks like she's ready to throttle me in anticipation. "Okay, just tell me already!"

"So, before I even hacked Dot, I swiped a vial of RRB and studied it under my portable microscope. Something jumped out at me right away when I looked in the lens. The radiation-resistant bacteria had a *nucleus*. And not just one or two, but three nuclei."

Sydney's head snaps up so fast, she could give herself whiplash. She knows as well as I do that there is no bacteria on Earth that contains a nucleus; it's as much a law of science as the law of gravity. So to find a strain of bacteria with three nuclei . . . means it's from another world.

"After that discovery, I knew my next step was to find evidence of biosignatures from Europa, to prove that life does exist there, and to find out its connection to the RRB. And the only realistic way I could think of for getting my hands on that data was through the robots."

Sydney gives me a sideways look.

"I don't know whether I should be freaked out by you, or impressed."

"I guess you can be both?" I say with a sheepish grin.

"So how did you possibly hack into Dot?" she presses. "We all assumed it was some sort of high-up cybercriminal."

"Er, not exactly. It's a long story that involves my own hacking software, and taking advantage of a golden opportunity to sneak into the robotics lab when you were all in the emergency tunnel the night of the storm. But in short, my plan worked. And when I programmed Dot with the command to show me any data she had for biosignatures on Europa . . . well, she brought me this."

I reach into the pocket of my sweatshirt where I've carefully hidden the notes that I jotted down from memory: my closest account of all the letters, numbers, and symbols that flashed before me on Dot's touch screen that night in Houston. Sydney snatches the paper from my hands and holds it under the flashlight. I watch her eyes widen in disbelief as she takes in the sketch at the center of the page: a cell, with an unprecedented three nuclei. Just like the RRB. And right underneath is the formula that fills in the missing piece; that answers humanity's foremost question about Europa.

$$C_{55}H_{72}O_5N_4Mg\text{-}CH4\text{-}E_+$$

Chlorophyll-Methane-Europa

"*Chlorophyll and methane found on Europa*," Sydney reads, her voice a whisper.

"The biosignatures I was looking for." I shiver at the memory.

But a second later, Sydney is crumpling up the paper and tossing it back to me, a look of distrust on her face.

"How do I know you didn't just make this whole thing up? I have no reason to believe you."

"And I have no reason to lie!" I protest.

"You could be playing a joke on me, or maybe this is some sort of . . . hazing ritual." Sydney folds her arms over her chest. "I'm not falling for it."

"Why can't you just consider the fact that I'm telling the truth? The RRB we've been injecting is *alive*, just like Suki tried telling me before she was sent away." I can feel myself growing desperate—if I can't convince our crew's medical expert, what hope do I have? "It's alive with the bacteria from Europa's extraterrestrial life, and it's changing us."

Sydney lets out a hollow laugh.

"And what kind of life are you suggesting? Because any

creature with three nuclei, that releases chlorophyll and methane and has a freaking tentacular club, would have to be some kind of monster."

"A tentacular what?"

I follow Sydney's pointed finger to one of the indecipherable images I'd seen flashing on Dot's touch screen and attempted to sketch from memory: an elongated, curved blade covered in clustered circles.

"Some of the things you're forced to study in premed biology, you wish you could forget," Sydney says darkly. "Like the semester spent on deep-sea gigantism, which included dissecting a giant squid. I swear, that terrifying thing gave me nightmares for a year." She looks at me indignantly. "That's how I know you're making this up. Because *that*"—she slaps the paper—"looks exactly like the two tentacular clubs on the giant squid, suckers and all." She points to the circles covering the curve, and I shake my head in disbelief. It never would have even occurred to me that that's what it was.

"I had no clue," I tell her. "And I really doubt the same giant squids that we have on Earth are popping up on Europa. Whatever is there, it's going to be different."

But it could be similar. It could look like a giant squid, and be just as violent and frightening to encounter.

And then another thought rushes in that turns my insides cold.

"What if—what if that's one of the reasons you were

chosen? Because they knew we might encounter these— these similar creatures, and you're the one with experience?"

"Stop it." Sydney jumps off the bed, but this time her expression is more fear than fury. "I've had enough of this conversation. I don't believe you, and honestly—I don't want to."

I stand up, feeling thisclose to tears.

"Should have known," I mutter, heading for the door. And as it starts sliding closed behind me, I hear Sydney call my name. But I don't look back.

At breakfast the next morning, I'm greeted by five bleary-eyed, dazed faces. It's clear my crewmates got about as much sleep as I did last night. It was impossible to relax in my tight quarters, with the feel of the walls closing in around me and the drone of foreign sounds, from the hum of our life-support systems to the whir of computer exhausts. Supposedly the sounds of space become like white noise for astronauts once they've been up here long enough—but I can't imagine anything ever feeling normal about this.

No one eats much of our vacuum-sealed, reheated bacon and eggs, and the conversation is equally sparse. I make a point of avoiding both Sydney's and Beckett's eyes, with the disheartening realization that I am friendless here. It's a relief when the ship's internal clock chimes the new hour, and I can push back from the table, with all of us due in the Communications Bay to upload the first of our daily instructions from Houston. My pulse quickens at the thought of the messages waiting for me—there has to be something new from home, and I still haven't heard anything from Leo—until I remember that the servers don't upload any personal mail until our "free time," hours from now. I let out a frustrated sigh before sitting down at the largest of the touch-screen desks, the one reserved for communications and technology specialist.

EIGHT (8) NEW FILES FROM HOUSTON MCC, a bubble onscreen reads. *PERMISSION TO UPLOAD?*

I click to accept, and the others crowd around me as we wait for the documents to load. The first six file names are self-explanatory—separate checklists for each of us—but it's the seventh that catches my eye.

"'*The Final Six*, Episode 1,'" I read aloud. "What the heck is that?"

"Must be the docuseries on us," Beckett says over my shoulder. "It's supposed to air weekly on all the major news channels across the world. Go on, play it."

I roll my eyes and press the button, and the cinema screen on the wall above us flickers to life. Sweeping music starts playing over a breathless montage, showing the six of us landing on the helipad for our training camp arrivals, juxtaposed with the moment when each of us learned we'd been chosen in the final draft. My heart stops at the split-second shot of me standing next to Leo on the Johnson Space Center steps, a shared agony reflected in both of our faces when my name is called without his. The montage moves on, the music growing more epic as the scene shifts to the rocket rising above the launchpad, but I'm still back on the steps with Leo—my heart shredding into pieces all over again.

The poised, commanding faces of Dr. Takumi and General Sokolov fill the screen next, as they sit across the *Newsline* desk in front of anchor Robin Richmond.

"Shouldn't they be too preoccupied worrying about our safety to go on a publicity tour?" I grumble, but Minka shushes me, leaning forward to hear what they have to say. The interview starts with Takumi and the general making the usual grandiose statements about the magnitude of what we're accomplishing, how it's the honor and privilege of their lifetimes to be leading the six of us, yada yada, with of course zero mention of any extraterrestrials or dangers waiting for us on Europa.

I get up, turning my back on the screen as my mind returns to those last moments with Leo. Until I hear the words *"pairing up the astronauts,"* and my spine stiffens. That better not mean what I think it does.

"Well, yes, of course. There's a reason we chose an equal number of each gender."

I turn around to see Dr. Takumi's lips curving up in a smile that doesn't suit him.

"The benefit of this extended journey on the *Pontus* is that it gives our space colonists time to get to know one another, form connections, and see who they are compatible with before officially partnering," he continues, as bile rises in my throat. "In several years—our estimates range from five to ten—Europa should be able to support new human life, at which time we will recommend the first conceptions."

"Oh my God." I stare at the screen, aghast.

"That's so unbelievably hetero of them, assuming we'd even want to partner up like that," Minka says, wrinkling her nose in disgust. We've finally found something we can agree on. "What century is this supposed to be, the twentieth?"

"No one can make you, or any of us, do it," I tell her. "We'll be on solid ground by then, away from their control."

"Yeah, but that's exactly when you'll *want* to procreate. It doesn't matter how you feel about any of us," Beckett says, and I give him an incredulous look. Did he really just say that?

"It's all biological," he continues breezily. "Five to ten years as one of only six people in the world, and trust me—biology is bound to kick in, and you'll be desperate to add new life."

"We'll never be that desperate," I shoot back.

"Ouch," Jian says wryly, and I can tell from his expression that he's only half kidding. But at this point, I don't care whose feelings I might have hurt. The only thing I'm actually desperate for is a way out.

"I wonder why they didn't tell us about this sooner," Dev says, staring back at the screen.

"It was always implied, though, wasn't it?" Sydney takes a step closer to him, as if subconsciously claiming Dev for herself.

She's right. Deep down I knew this was the expected outcome, and Leo had known it too. It added another wrenching layer to our good-bye. And now, as I try to imagine pairing up with one of the guys here—all I can feel is the sting of dismay.

Message Origin: *** CAUTION—ID
UNKNOWN ***
Message Recipient: *PONTUS* Spacecraft—
Earth-Mars Transit
Attn: ARDALAN, NAOMI
[Message Status: Received—Encrypted]

Dear Naomi,

I wish I could have written you sooner, and that this message could tell you everything I need and want to say. There's so much I want to share, and I will as soon as I can—but I have to disappear for a while. I promise it's for a good reason, one that I think—hope—you'll feel is worth it. I'm going to miss your words and your voice, your eyes and your smile, even more than I already do now.

I wanted you to have something of me for the weeks ahead, when I'm not able to video-chat or write. This song was my mom's favorite, and now that I'm older, I finally understand the lyrics. They describe how I feel about you.

Te voglio bene assai.

Leo

SEVEN

LEO

"HERE WE GO. YOU READY?"

I look over at Asher sitting next to me in the virtual reality flight simulator, and I grin.

"Ready."

My seat shoots back into the reclined position, my legs at ninety degrees. A three-screen tablet unfurls above me at eye level, while a piloting hand controller slides under my palm. I click the blinking green triangle on-screen to start the automatic ground launch sequencer, which Asher just taught me how to use, and call out, "We're a go for auto sequence start." I pause. "I'm supposed to activate something next, right?"

"The main engine hydrogen burnoff system," Asher

says, reaching overhead to show me the command on the touch-screen panel.

"Ground launch sequencer commanding main engine start," a smooth, automated female voice echoes from inside the cockpit. "Five . . . four . . . three . . ."

The vibrations pummel the flight capsule, rattling and shaking all four walls, as the engine roars to life. I have to strain to hear Asher's voice in my headset above the noise, while I use the hand controller to throttle the main engine up and down.

"Approaching main engine cutoff!" Asher calls. He joins in the countdown: ". . . Two—one!"

Suddenly my body is flying forward in its seat, my safety straps the only thing keeping me from bursting through the window shield. I let out a whoop as a wild surge of adrenaline floods through me, my stomach flipping upside down, my skin turning numb from the speed.

"Entering MAX-Q!"

I refocus on the screens, remembering from the lecture Asher gave me over breakfast that this is the most dangerous part of launch—when the ship reaches maximum pressure from the outside air rushing past the speed of sound. "One . . . two . . ."

I'm already holding my breath before he gets to three. Just one more step, and the launch sim is complete. But then my body slams to the side as the ship makes a sudden swerve.

"What was th—"

I break off as the capsule lurches back and forth, like an angry animal trying to shake us loose. And then it starts spinning wildly, and my fingers are fumbling with the tablet screen in front of me but we're moving too fast, I can't see—

"It's a malfunctioned maneuvering thruster!" Asher shouts, scanning his screen. "To regain control, we need you to go into the main altitude control system and—"

The capsule makes a sudden swoop, starting to nose-dive, and I cut Asher off with a yell.

"Wrong direction, wrong direction!"

I jab at the controls on the touch screen, but now we're pitching down at too great a speed, the ground looming closer than the sky. I push on the hand controller, I try to reignite the rockets, but a blinking red alarm alerts me of our insufficient fuel. We must have used up the amount needed on the ascent, and now that we're plummeting, there's no going back up.

"Looks like we're headed for an emergency water landing," Asher says grimly. "Aim for the section of the ocean that's highlighted on the screen in front of you, then decelerate once your wheels align with the water. And don't forget to deploy the parachutes."

I grip the hand control, my stomach sinking along with our ship as I steer us toward the last place I intended. And then our capsule comes slamming to a stop, splashing down on the water with an impact that nearly yanks us from our seats. A slow *beep* echoes through the capsule, and Asher pulls off his VR headset.

"Well, you crashed the sim, but on the bright side, you probably didn't die."

I groan, tearing off my headset.

"That was embarrassing. I completely failed that test."

"Let's just hope there won't be any *actual* malfunctioning thrusters on Dr. Wagner's ship." He gives me a reassuring grin. "Don't worry. We'll keep practicing until you know how to troubleshoot your way out of almost anything."

"There's no time for that."

Asher and I jump as a third voice fills our headsets. I wonder how long Greta's been listening, and if my performance was as much a disappointment to her as it was to me.

"I need you two to see something. Meet me in my upstairs office. Now."

Asher raises an eyebrow.

"This should be interesting."

We climb out of the training capsule and run up the stairs to Greta's real office, the one overlooking her underground lab, rather than the public-facing show office in the main compound. My palms grow sweaty the closer we get to her door, where we find her deep in conversation with Lark, both of them staring at the monitor mounted above her touch-screen desk.

"What's wrong?" I blurt out.

My question is answered as soon as I follow their eyes to the screen. It's *me*—my photo alongside Lark's and Asher's, with a ticking news alert flashing underneath. "EUROPA MISSION FINALISTS, TRAINER, MISSING."

"Damn," Asher says under his breath. "That was fast."

The image shifts to two familiar figures standing at the top of the ISTC campus steps, their faces like stone as they stare into a crowd of cameras and flashbulbs. My throat turns dry as Dr. Takumi starts to speak.

"It has unfortunately come to our attention that two eliminated finalists—who, incidentally, were roommates during their time at Space Training Camp—have gone missing, along with a member of our faculty. We have reason to believe this may be an act of retaliation against the ISTC over their eliminations, and we can only speculate that they've taken their former team leader against her will."

What? I recoil in disbelief. Of all the ways I imagined them handling our disappearance, I never predicted this. I guess I didn't give them enough credit for being this cold, this mercenary.

"How transparent," Greta mutters. "I know they've figured out by now who you're aligned with. This is just a stunt, trying to publicly shame you three into abandoning our plans."

"We are calling on you, global citizens, to contact us if you have *any* information on their whereabouts," the general says, her voice dripping with fake sincerity. "And of course, if any of these three individuals are spotted, they must be apprehended and brought to local authorities at once."

Asher sinks into the nearest chair, and I feel a crush of guilt that my friend—who earned honors for his piloting in the Israeli Defense Forces, and has been nothing but good his entire life—is now a target, with his reputation smeared. All because of me.

"That's it," I declare. "You two should get out of here now—show yourselves, let the press know you were never missing and that it's all a big misunderstanding. Whatever training is left, Dr. Wagner and I can handle it."

"No way," Lark says. "All coming forward will do is give Takumi and Sokolov access to us, and they'll hunt us till they get the answers they want. About you, Dr. Wagner, everything. Not to mention what they'll do to me for jumping ship."

"She's right," Asher says, giving me a brave half smile. "And besides, anyone who really knows us and hears that story . . . they won't believe it."

I rake my hands through my hair, feeling beyond helpless.

"I'm sorry, guys."

"What we need to focus on now is how to truncate your training so you can depart sooner than planned, possibly as early as this weekend," Greta says, her words giving me a fresh jolt of adrenaline. "Now that there's heat on us, we can't afford extra time on the ground—"

She breaks off midsentence, her eyes flying to the band around her wrist as it starts flashing with pulses of red light. And then a robot's voice, one that sounds like Corion, echoes through the room.

"Police at main gate. Do you copy? Police at *main* gate. We couldn't fend them off this time. Beginning intruder protocols now."

I freeze in place. This isn't happening. Not now, not when I'm so close, not to my friends—

"Over here!" Greta directs us, and I spring into motion, following her to the wall farthest from the door. She runs her palm over one of the wall panels, and I watch as yet another camouflaged space juts forward, this one some type of supply closet. She pushes the three of us inside, where there's only inches of room to hide out alongside vials and lab instruments. I hear Greta's footsteps grow fainter, and then it's just the three of us, balancing our weight in the cramped, dark space.

No one says a word, even though we're clearly alone. The only sounds are of our muffled breathing and the hum of the room's electronics, until Lark lets out a gasp.

"They're coming," she whispers, staring down at a red-flashing wristband identical to Greta's. Light pulses through it, spelling a Morse code message in the dark. "Don't let anyone hear you breathe."

And then, on cue, we hear the swing of the door as it flies open. Several sets of footsteps come thundering into Greta's office, and I can hear my own heartbeat now, clanging so loudly in my ears that I'm sure it'll give us away. I feel nails digging into my arm and I turn to see Asher, his face a mask of panic.

We can hear Greta fuming at the officers, talking a mile a minute, first in German and then in English.

"This is absolutely ludicrous. You have no evidence, nothing that gives you the right—"

"In here!" one of the men yells, and my heart stops. *They found us—it's over.* Instead of joining Naomi on Europa, I'm going to be trapped in a jail cell—

Someone is flinging open drawers, shoving papers to the floor. That's when I realize it's not us that they found.

"Care to explain this?" one of the men barks.

"Just—examining a theory," Greta says stiffly. "It turned out to be false."

Something in her tone tells me that whatever they're looking at, the policeman wasn't supposed to see. If only the closet had slats so I could find out what it is . . . But then we hear the footsteps changing direction, moving away from us, out of the room. And I can breathe again.

It's fifteen minutes before Greta rejoins us. I know because I was staring at Lark's blinking wristband the entire time, wondering with each passing minute if Greta wasn't coming back; if they'd found something to arrest her for. Finally we hear her voice on the other side of the door, sounding both drained and triumphant.

"They're gone. I managed to convince them that you three have nothing to do with Wagner Enterprises."

"Well done." Asher exhales as she opens the closet door, letting us out. "I thought we were goners."

"Not today. But it's only a matter of time before they come back, likely with Takumi and Sokolov in tow," Greta says, her mouth set in a thin line. "Which means we need to revisit the discussion about launching Leo well ahead of schedule, so that all three of you can be out of here by the time the government figures out exactly what we're up to."

"Let's do it." I stand up straighter, filled with determination. "Let's launch as soon as we can. Tomorrow."

"Whoa. Dude." Asher coughs. "I mean, you did just crash the last flight sim. I know you'll be ready eventually, but not *that* fast. I say we continue the training schedule we'd planned."

"I'll practice all night, then," I reply, thinking fast. "I'll even sleep in the simulator! I just . . . can't risk missing this, if they come back and find us next time."

Greta looks between the two of us carefully.

"One more full day of training, and then we will reassess," she decides. "I'm not sending anyone to space unprepared. But the longer we wait, the greater our risk."

My stomach knots as I realize the subtext behind her words.

If I can't be ready by tomorrow, I may not end up going at all. And if we get caught before I make it to launch—then my future isn't the only one that will go up in flames.

I haven't had a single shot of RRB since the night before I was cut from the draft, so it sends a shock wave through me when I see the familiar blue serum swirling inside the syringe in Greta's hands. It's after dinner, and just the two of us remain in her office. Lark and Asher have already gone to their rooms for the night, but she asked me to stay.

"I would have thought you'd be against injecting this— this stuff," I blurt out as she reaches over to roll up my sleeve.

"I developed this 'stuff,'" she answers calmly, and I pull my arm back in surprise.

"But—but then that means *you're* responsible for what happened to Callum and Suki. Weren't they part of the reason Lark left ISTC in the first place? How could you ever think injecting alien bacteria is a good idea?"

My head spins, as once again my confidence in Greta and this whole situation is shaken.

"I would have recognized that their bodies could not withstand it had I been given the opportunity to review their DNA sequencing," Greta says crisply. "But by the time Takumi and Sokolov chose them for the initial group of finalists, I was already off the mission. And the doses you all received at ISTC were significantly higher than I prescribed."

DNA sequencing. My mind slips back to the other night, and I wonder if that's what she was doing—checking my DNA to make sure I could handle the RRB. But why the coded messaging?

"To answer your second question," Greta continues, "this alien bacteria is the only shield we've got—and not just from radiation." She meets my eyes with a firm gaze. "Now hold still."

This time I don't move away. But as the RRB seeps through my veins, so does a growing sense of unease.

Cold fingers are running down my neck. Someone is breathing behind me, the same person whose clothes I've been wearing. He doesn't like it, doesn't like that I'm here. And then I see another face behind him, one that's been missing for too long. It's my sister, Angelica, crying out to warn me.

I wake up with a gasp and find my shirt soaked in sweat, despite the cold chills running through my body, making me shiver uncontrollably. For a second I have the crushing thought that I'm getting sick and Greta will be forced to cut me from the mission, since only astronauts in perfect health get launched into space. But then I feel the tenderness on my arm, and remember the shot. It's only side effects. The first injection is always the worst.

The dream is harder to shake off—it had an urgency to it that felt so *real*. After ten minutes of tossing and turning, I give up on sleep and climb out of bed. A small voice in my head, one that sounds an awful lot like Naomi's, urges me to sneak back up to Greta's private floor and see if I can get my questions answered, but I settle for killing time in the guest floor lounge instead. With the way my body feels, I don't think I have it in me to do much investigating right now.

But when I get to the lounge and see the row of framed photographs sitting on the piano, my pulse quickens. Maybe somewhere among them, I'll find a clue?

Before I know it, I'm riffling through the picture frames, hunting for the face from the bedroom upstairs. To my disappointment, it's one photo after another of Greta with different Nobel Prize winners and world leaders. There's not a single sign of a personal life here.

"Leo? What are you doing?"

My head snaps up at the sound of Lark's voice. I turn around and find her standing in the doorway in a robe and slippers, her eyebrows knitting together as she watches me.

"Um, I—couldn't sleep," I answer, wincing at the thought of her reporting this scene to Greta in the morning. "Sorry, did I wake you?"

"Well, you were banging around in here," she says wryly. Her eyes flit to the frames. "Looking for something?"

I hesitate. Just as I'm about to fib my way through this, it occurs to me that Lark might be the closest I can get to the truth.

"Did you know Greta has a son? What happened to him?"

Her mouth falls open.

"I—that's not what I was expecting you to say."

"Tell me."

Lark's eyes dart back and forth, as if Greta could be within earshot.

"It's sensitive—I shouldn't be talking about it. She's never even spoken to me about him. I only know because of—of what happened the same week as the *Athena* disaster." She fidgets with the ring around her finger anxiously, and it's only then that I realize it's a diamond. An engagement ring from the fiancé she lost on the mission.

"He died—didn't he?"

Lark nods and my stomach coils. For some reason, I

can't help viewing my fate as linked to his.

"His bedroom upstairs . . . everything is untouched from five years ago, like she thinks he's coming back," I blurt out. "Believe me, I know what grief is like. I also know it can make you—not *right* sometimes, mentally. I've been there myself." I take a deep breath. "I want to go to Europa, there's no question about that. But I need to know how much of what she's telling me is real—or in her head."

Lark smiles sadly.

"It's both, Leo. Every proven scientific fact was once a wild idea or hypothesis in someone's head. The only thing that makes it 'real' is proof, and in our case, that proof can only come from you."

She's right, I know. I'm not expecting her to say anything more, but she glances at me with compassion, and then starts to speak in a low voice.

"His name was Johannes. Greta kept him shielded from the public eye because she always feared him becoming a target, but those in her inner circle knew he was the center of her world. Everyone thinks of Dr. Wagner as being totally work obsessed, and she is, but she also always wanted a child. And as time went on, it started to look less likely. She'd had a few relationships, all with women, but nothing lasting. It's hard to be in a relationship with a genius who's always preoccupied. I know that myself." Lark glances down at her ring. "Anyway. She eventually found a donor and had her baby, and for eighteen years, things were good."

"So then what happened?"

"Johannes always wanted to be involved in Greta's work, and she mentored him from an early age to follow in her footsteps. When Wagner Enterprises completed production on a new fusion-powered spacecraft, he lobbied hard to take the first flight. All the preliminary checks looked good, and Johannes had flown to the ISS before, so Greta agreed to let him take the new ship on a test flight there. What happened next was—" Lark's voice catches. "It was a freak accident. The air braking system used for atmospheric reentry deployed prematurely, and the ship . . . it disintegrated in flight."

I cover my mouth in horror. The room starts to sway around me.

"Greta was destroyed over it. And then, it was only a few days later that the *Athena* went dark." Lark turns away from me now, and it's a few moments before she can speak again.

"We were all shattered by it, but the NASA leaders at the time pushed the blame for *Athena* onto Greta. It's the reason they cut ties and canceled all their contracts with Wagner Enterprises. Leadership said she was too grief-stricken over Johannes to do her job monitoring the mission, and must have missed something. Even I, who *needed* someone to blame, knew that was completely unfair. I mean, there was a whole SatCon team monitoring the *Athena*, too. It wasn't just her."

My head is spinning. Greta's son didn't just die—he died

on her mission, her spacecraft. And I'm about to walk into his footsteps.

"I always felt for her, after that," Lark continues. "Greta lost everything that mattered to her in the span of a week. The way she coped was by drowning herself in her own work. That's around the time she started the *Space Conspirator*, and became more and more consumed by what Dr. Takumi called 'fringe theories.' When the Europa Mission was greenlit, she tried reconnecting with the ISTC to warn them about the likelihood of extraterrestrial life. But Dr. Takumi and the general just wrote it off as the ravings of a scientist whose tragedy had turned her 'mad.'"

"You believe her, though." I look closely at Lark. "You wouldn't be here otherwise."

"I do," she says simply. "The science is all sound. And I think someone who went through what she did is more likely to tell the truth than anyone on the other side. She has nothing left to lose."

"Do you think . . ." My voice falters. I don't know how to phrase what I want to say without coming across like too much of a coward. "Do you think it's safe, what she's planning for me? Or could I be another . . . tragic story like him?"

Lark puts her hand on my arm.

"If I thought that, I wouldn't be here trying to help you go. If anything, the Wagner ships are that much more carefully constructed and perfected after Johannes's accident." She pauses. "But I also know the old NASA motto is true:

'Risk is the price of progress.' There are no guarantees."

"I know."

It's the chance that I said I was willing to take. So now it's time to stand by my words—and just hope I can end up with the reward instead of the risk.

EIGHT

NAOMI

TODAY, OUR SEVENTH DAY IN SPACE, IS THE FIRST MORNING I
wake up knowing where I am. Instead of instinctively calling out for my mom and dad, or expecting to open my eyes
and see my space camp dorm room, this time there's no shot
of surprise when the lights flick on. I know that the slightly
annoying pop song I hear isn't coming from my phone, or
Sam's room, but from Mission Control. I know that when
I roll over in bed and pull up the window shade to look
outside, it'll be more about what isn't there than what is.
No ground beneath us, no clouds above us. Just the never-
ending stretch of black. So I guess I can say I'm making
progress in the "seven stages of Earth-grieving" that our
NASA psychologist lectured us about before we left. I've

officially crossed out of Denial.

It probably helps that, one week in, our days on the *Pontus* have fallen into something of a pattern. Mornings start with breakfast as a team, while Dr. Takumi or General Sokolov joins in over the squawk box telecom to run through the day's agenda. Usually we'll have one big VR training simulation as a group—a multisensory rehearsal of our upcoming Mars maneuver, or troubleshooting a hypothetical emergency—followed by a block of solo training and tasks around the ship tailored to each of our specific roles. My role as communications and technology specialist means I spend a few hours each day alone under a pair of heavy-duty headphones in the Communications Bay, interfacing with NASA and the Europa Mission leaders, downloading uplinks from Earth, and deciphering any coded messages that come in from the International Space Station or other satellites in orbit. When I pretend that it's not forever—that I'm just living out my grandest science-nerd fantasy, and can go home whenever I want—then the truth is that I love what I do here. But even then, beneath the thrill of cracking codes and standing at the helm of all this next-level tech, is a quiet that gets under your skin. Space camp was a bustling hub of people and activity, a place where you never felt alone, no matter how hard the homesickness hit. Here, we might as well be wearing our isolation like a uniform. All it takes is a glance out the window to know we're fatally far from everything we know and love.

Dinner is when the six of us regroup, and as I zip up the

elevator pod after three hours of tracking satellite signals, I'm craving human conversation almost as much as food. But I'm the last arrival in the dining room, where I find my crewmates split up into two tables: Sydney, Dev, and Jian in one camp, and Beckett and Minka in the other. I'm obviously not about to sit with Beckett, but as Sydney and I make uneasy eye contact across the room, I can tell she doesn't want me at her table, either.

It feels like junior high all over again, only this time there's no escape. I grab my tray and slide into an empty table alone, pulling a notebook and pen out of my back-pack. At least I can pretend I chose to sit by myself, that I have things to do. I start jotting down a message to type up for Sam before bed, but I'm soon distracted by the sound of Dev's and Sydney's chuckling.

"You weirdo," I hear her call him fondly, like it's the biggest compliment.

I squeeze my eyes shut, imagining for a moment that things played out the way they were supposed to—that instead of sitting alone, I'm next to Leo, and it's his laugh I hear. And then it hits me that I can't even really *remember* his laugh, even though it's only been, what, ten days since we were separated? Maybe if I'd had a voice or video message from him by now, it would be less hazy . . . but he's been more silent than I want to admit.

"Hey. You okay?"

I glance up at the sound of Jian, who's stopped by my table on the way to dump his empty tray.

"Yeah." I manage a smile. "Just . . . tired, I guess."

"Well, if you're up for it, you should join us for a movie tonight," he says. "We're screening an old classic I think you'd like. *Hidden Figures*."

"That's my favorite, actually."

I was hooked on that movie even before I saw the first frame, just from Dad's description back when I was ten. *"It's about women whose brainpower changed the future of science and space travel. That's the kind of woman I know you can grow up to be, azizam."*

"Good. So you'll be there?" Jian grins.

I push away the pang of loneliness for my dad, for home.

"Yeah. See you in a bit."

"Naomi. You've got to see this."

My body stiffens at the sound of Beckett's voice as I step into the living room, a den-like space on the top floor of our Astronauts' Residence, with a couple of bolted-down couches and armchairs facing a cinema screen. I almost bailed on joining them up here—there's something a little less lonely about being by myself with a good book than surrounded by five people I don't belong with. But then I thought of Jian's kind expression, and I forced myself into the elevator pod. Now, though, with Beckett's voice like a threat, I wish I'd followed my first instinct.

"I thought you guys were watching *Hidden Figures*." I squint at the screen, where a grave-faced anchorwoman addresses the camera. "Why is the news on?"

"Trust me," says the last person I would ever trust. "You don't want to miss this."

And then I see him. *Leo*. His deep blue eyes and dimpled smile fill the screen, reaching straight into my heart. For one horrendous moment, I think the worst has happened to him, and I imagine myself running out to the airlock, throwing off my helmet, giving myself to space.

But then Lark's face and Asher's join the frame, and the air whooshes from my lungs. They must be together somewhere.

"Rumors are swirling about the missing Europa finalists, where they've gone, and *why* they've taken an ISTC employee with them," the anchorwoman says, her voice dripping with drama. "Stay tuned at the top of the hour for an exclusive statement from Dr. Ren Takumi—"

I turn away from the TV, not wanting to hear a thing he has to say. The others are watching me, gauging my reaction, and I force a tight smile on my face.

"There's a good explanation for this. I know it."

"Naomi—" I hear Jian start to say, but I don't wait for him to finish. I'm already running, out of the room and into the elevator pod, my stomach dropping as it swoops me down to the Communications Bay. If ever I needed a message from Leo, it's now.

My legs practically fly to the nearest touch-screen desk, where I swipe my thumbprint and log in to my email in the span of a breath. All week, I've been telling myself that his silence must be just because of the tenuous Wi-Fi situation back in Rome—but what if it means something else?

The sight of the boldfaced new message at the top of my inbox fills my eyes with relieved tears. *He's okay. He's safe.*

He didn't forget me.

I reread Leo's words twice, my eyes lingering on the sentence about him having to disappear for a while and his promise that it's all for a good reason. I don't know how I can possibly wait to find out what he and Lark and Asher are up to, and I feel a pang of regret that I'm not there—not a part of it.

I click on the song file he included with his message, and a stirring voice and melody break the silence in the room.

"Te voglio bene assai,
ma tanto tanto bene sai."

My cheeks fill with heat as I recognize what the first lines of the chorus mean. *"I love you very much, you know."* As I take in every note, every chord, I can almost feel Leo sitting beside me, murmuring the same words in my ear.

I'm dying to understand the rest of the lyrics after my first listen, and I quickly enter the song into the translator app on my desk. My breath catches as the English rendition appears, describing feelings I never dreamed anyone would attribute to . . . me.

Everything else falls away—the ship, the rest of the six, the loneliness in here, the terrors waiting out there. For one magical moment, all I hear and see is him. And even though we're worlds apart, even though we'll never stand in the same room again . . . for as long as the song plays, I feel like the luckiest girl in the universe.

I don't even remember getting back to my room that night; I was in such a giddy daze. The logical side of my brain tried to poke through my bubble, reminding me that this is a love story without a happy ending. But for once, I let my emotional—possibly delusional—side win. I went to bed still floating, his song still playing in my head. So it was that much more jarring when I woke up in the middle of the night to the sound of urgent knocking.

I pull the covers up to my chest like a shield. *What time is it?* I riffle through the bedside shelf for my tablet and switch it on, the numbers on-screen blinking through the dark: 03:15:08 UTC. A decidedly creepy time of night for someone to come lurking by my door.

The knocking starts up again, but this time I hear a pattern—an almost rhythmic series of taps. I close my eyes, focusing in on the length of each tap, matching it to a letter in the Morse alphabet. S. Y. D—

I grab the flashlight next to my bed and jump up, stumbling toward the door. Sure enough, I find Sydney on the other side, dressed in sweats and clutching a flashlight of her own. As the light reflects against her face, I catch her expression—frozen with panic.

"What's wrong?" I motion her inside, but she doesn't move. "I thought you were done talking to me."

"I tested the RRB," Sydney whispers. "I didn't want to believe you, but I couldn't stop thinking about what you said. So I decided to check it out for myself, only I . . . took it a step further."

"What do you mean?" I stare at her.

"Just come with me. I need you to see something, before all the lights and cameras come back on in the morning."

"Okay . . . Give me a second."

I rummage through the drawer under my bed for a pair of socks and a hoodie to throw on over my pj's, and then I follow her through the sliding door of my compartment. A wall of darkness is waiting, and my hands shake as I aim the flashlight higher, its thin glow barely penetrating.

"C'mon." Sydney grips my arm, and we take slow, careful steps toward the elevator pod. And then, once we're close enough for the pod to register our footsteps, it lights up with its silvery glow, giving us a break from the dark. I breathe a sigh of relief as we step inside.

"Where are we going, exactly?" I ask Sydney.

"The Floating Lab," she answers, and I raise my eyebrows. So far, only our science officer, aka Minka, and mission medical officer, Sydney, have been granted access to the lab. I was wondering when it would be my turn. Knowing my track record, I probably should have guessed that I'd end up sneaking my way in.

We bump past the row of touch-screen desks in the Communications Bay, moving toward the hatch door that leads us out of our Astronauts' Residence bubble and onto the humanless, uncharted side of the ship. Sydney aims our flashlights forward while I yank open the hatch, and as we crawl inside, through the tunnel that connects all the different modules of the ship—our bodies start to rise. There's a rush in my stomach, the air escapes my lungs, as zero gravity returns. It's a feeling I can't imagine ever getting used to.

We propel ourselves forward by pushing off handholds, floating past the artificial greenhouse, the payload bay, and the storage module until we get to the airlock that leads to the lab. I follow Sydney through the heavy circular door and wave my flashlight ahead, catching glimpses of a working zero g science lab through the pale beam of light. Wires coil from floor to ceiling, fold-down lab tables extend from the walls, monitor screens and magnifying mirrors swivel above our heads, and at least two dozen science instruments wait within arm's reach, secured to a Velcro partition of the wall. I'm so fixated on our surroundings that, for a second, I forget the real reason we're here.

Until Sydney presses her palms against a padded white section of the wall, which swings open to reveal a lab fridge. She pulls out a glass petri dish, the bottom of it filled with a familiar blue liquid. And then she pushes the middle of one of the folded-up lab tables till it springs into working position, grabs a microscope off one of the wall shelves, and practically pushes me in front of it, where I cling to a handrail to keep from floating away. Watching Sydney in action, it occurs to me that I might have been wrong before, thinking I didn't belong with the others here. I'm clearly not the only one willing to break the rules and put myself in dicey situations, all in the name of science—and the truth.

"You were right about the three nuclei," Sydney murmurs behind me as I adjust the lens. "Once I saw that, I was . . . well, freaked-out would be an understatement. All I could think was that I had to know what *kind* of life this bizarro cell represents if I'm going to keep giving us these injections. So then I thought, if you were right about the RRB coming from Europa, I could try replicating the atmospheric conditions of Europa on the microscopic level. I just changed the temperature of the water in the petri dish and mixed it with nutrients and a spare amount of oxygen and carbon—"

My stomach comes crashing to the floor.

"You *just* did all that? Sydney, please tell me you didn't reanimate something when we don't even know what it is!"

Her silence confirms my fears. And as I lean into the lens, I can feel every muscle in my body tensing, bracing for the unknown.

At first glance, it looks no different from the bacteria I saw under my own microscope when I investigated the RRB back at space camp: a reddish tube-shaped organism, with its unprecedented three nuclei in the middle of the cell's cytoplasm. And then—

I let out a scream, recoiling so fast that I lose my grip on the handrail. The dormant bacteria is *twitching*—once, then twice. And then it pounces to life. Six spindly tendrils sprout around its exterior, like limbs, and suddenly its tube-like shell is doubling in size, expanding right there beneath the glass.

I spring backward in shock, the zero g sending me flying straight into the wall. I find a ladder to grasp on to and Sydney joins me on the other side, the two of us staring down at the abandoned lab table in fear.

"I didn't just see that," I say when I find my voice.

"It did the same thing with me, too," Sydney says shakily. "But when I looked a second time, that . . . that *thing* had gone down to its normal size. So it must have the ability to change its size and shape at will."

"That's not terrifying or anything." I gulp. My body turns cold as it hits me just how alone Sydney and I are in here, with an unknown specimen growing as we speak. It takes every ounce of self-control to think clearly, to not just sprint out of the lab.

"We need to confront the mission leaders about this. But first—we can't let that thing continue growing when we're all confined together on this ship. We have to . . ." My voice trails off because of course it's the last thing I want to say. A discovery like this, a new form of life, is a scientist's miracle. And I'm about to suggest killing it.

"I thought you might say that." Sydney drops her eyes to the floor. "I'm sorry I got us into this mess. I should have just believed you."

Um, yeah you should have. But I swallow the retort, forcing myself to remain calm. Besides, I'm not really one to talk, not after what I did to Dot.

"It's okay. Let's just figure out what to do. I'm thinking our best option is to . . . dump it out the main airlock," I say with a wince. "The one leading out into space."

"That means suiting up for a spacewalk," Sydney says. "How will we manage all that with just the two of us and a couple of flashlights? Not to mention, the airlock is so close to the flight capsule."

"Right. Cyb." I sigh heavily. Chances are the robot is still plugged into his charging pod for the night, but if he happens to be awake and manning the cockpit, there's no way he won't hear us—and getting cornered by Dr. Takumi's AI crone would only make this night about ten times more complicated.

I aim the flashlight around the lab, the thin light circling the space as I search for something we might be able to use. And then I pause as the pale glow lands on a bolted-down black-and-white machine, taking up a third of the lab's north wall. It looks just like one of the vintage copy machines or printer/scanners back on Earth, but with an ironclad door securing what's inside, and a dozen more buttons on the outside.

"The catalytic oxidizer," I murmur. "That could work."

"Really?" Sydney follows my flashlight's beam with her eyes. "Have you used one of these before?"

"Not yet—it's really Minka's territory—but I know how it works. It's the device that uses a catalyst to decompose hazardous waste and convert it into methane gas for rocket fuel." I look up, feeling my spirits rise. "So once we put the petri dish inside, the machine's steaming, high-pressure air should kill the bacteria and turn it into methane!"

"You sure that's all it'll turn into?" Sydney asks, biting one of her fingernails.

"That's all the oxidizer is made to do," I tell her. "Besides, what other options do we have?"

"True." Sydney glances from the petri dish under the microscope to the oxidizer. "So all we have to do is get it inside?"

I nod. We both hesitate, neither of us particularly eager to go near the alien organism again. But then I take a deep breath and push off the ladder toward the lab table. It was my idea, after all.

Sydney follows, and I'm relieved when she makes the move toward the microscope, taking the petri dish in her hands. She keeps her eyes trained straight ahead, avoiding the scene within the glass, but her shallow gulps of breath let me know how scared she really is. I shine my flashlight on the petri dish, unable to stop myself from looking, and my heart jumps in my throat at the sight of skittering movement. Something as microscopic as bacteria cells should never be visible to the naked eye—which means the organism in Sydney's hands is growing at an exponential rate.

"Hurry," I say through gritted teeth, giving her a slight push forward in the air toward the machine.

It takes me another few minutes to figure out how to power on the machine, my heart hammering in my chest the whole time as I study the different buttons and acronyms on the display screen, all too aware of the ticking time bomb Sydney is holding. Finally the door opens with a pop, its interior already hissing with gathering steam.

"Here goes." I bite my lip, torn between relief and regret as Sydney gingerly slides the dish inside. My voice drops to a whisper as I look at the dark movement in the glass one last time. "I'm sorry . . ."

I tell myself a dozen different things as the machine whirs into motion and the petri dish starts spinning, dissolving. I tell myself that the organism could have been dangerous, that it could have threatened our ship, our mission, our lives. We had to do this. It was our duty. We couldn't afford to wait a moment longer and let the risk build.

But none of that diminishes my guilt. Because what if I'm wrong? What if it only *looks* freakish and threatening, but really isn't? What if we just killed a landmark scientific discovery for no reason?

The machine emits a series of beeps, and then a tube running from the back of the oxidizer into the ship's wall starts gurgling with activity. *The converted methane.* And a moment later, everything falls still. The sequence is complete.

Sydney and I exchange a nervous glance before I open the door to the oxidizer. Inside, there is no longer any hint of the RRB or petri dish. All that's left is the lingering steam.

"Well, that's probably the last time I reanimate something," Sydney says, breathing a sigh of relief.

"I should hope so." I glance down at my wrist monitor.

"C'mon, let's get out of here. Maybe we can still manage to get in a couple hours of sleep before the wake-up call."

We float across the lab to the hatch door, neither of us looking back as we close it behind us. We cross through the ship's modules in silence, and it's not until we open the door to the Astronauts' Residence and our feet hit the floor that things start to regain a smidge of normalcy. Riding back up the elevator pod together, Sydney gives my arm a squeeze.

"Thanks, Naomi. I owe you one. Or five." She pauses. "Friends?"

"Of course."

As unsettling as that whole adventure was, at least I have an ally here now—something I'm beginning to realize how much I needed.

We tiptoe off the elevator pod onto our floor, and I stop in front of my sleeping compartment.

"See you in the morning," I say through a yawn. "Goodnight, Sydney."

"Goodnight," she echoes. "Sleep well."

But as my mind replays the scene we just left, something tells me we'll be lucky to sleep at all.

NINE

FOR THE FIRST TIME SINCE I MET HER, GRETA WAGNER APPEARS nervous. I catch her eyeing me warily during our morning training and I can't help wondering if she's changed her mind—if she's figured out that I'm just a has-been athlete, not the astronaut prodigy she was hoping for. Her mind seems to be somewhere else while quizzing me on the different regions of Europa, and I brace myself for the blow I feel coming. I might have had my own reservations about putting my life in Greta's hands after what happened to Johannes, but the thought of her dropping me from the mission reminds me again how much I want this—*need* this.

And then I hear a howl, coming from the supposedly soundproof lab windows. *Wind.* In our new, climate-mangled

Earth, that sound never means anything good.

Greta's eyes dart back and forth, from me to the brewing storm clouds visible through the lab's skylight window. "We have to get you out of here before it hits."

True to her warning, we speed through the rest of my training day. From Cartography, where Greta shows me how to interpret and follow the hidden map crisscrossing Europa's surface, to Space Survival 101 with Lark and a flight training sim with Asher that I actually pass this time, it all flies by in fast-forward.

We're just sitting down for a quick meal in the lab, brought to us by Corion on a gleaming silver tray, when our conversation is cut short by the sound of the wind. It's been howling in the background all day, but this last gust is more like a scream, echoing at a pitch that could shatter glass.

We all look up to see darkness falling across the skylight window, even though it's only the middle of the day. Greta points to the wall, muttering something in German, and suddenly a video screen lowers over it, flickering with images from the news. That's when we see what's really happening outside—the clouds unleashing their fury once again.

I grip the side of the table with white knuckles, watching as the scene shifts from violently swaying trees to roofs ripping off their structures in Salzburg, just a couple of hours away from here. A map fills the screen, and as it zooms in on Vienna, the city outside our door, the footage flashes to the clouds swirling and funneling into something new.

"The tornado first made landfall in Munich and is moving swiftly east toward Vienna—"

Greta drops her plate with a clang. "The ship!"

She pushes back from the table and the rest of us follow suit, our chairs scraping against the metal floor as Corion shouts directions to his staff into a headset. "Engage the secondary barriers. Unlock the storm shelter!" He gestures for us to follow him, but after a split-second decision, I turn on my heel and make a run for the concealed cabinet Greta showed me. The one that holds my space suit and life-support pack.

"What are you doing?" I hear Asher yell behind me, but I don't stop moving until I'm in front of the hidden cabinet, pushing it open with my palm.

"Leo." Greta catches up to me, studying my face intently. "Are you certain?"

"We can't wait any longer," I answer. "I know this tornado could wreck our ship, or cost us our launch window, or both. Let me go now, while I still have a chance."

She hesitates, and for a moment I'm sure she's going to say no. But then she gives a slight nod, and starts calling out instructions.

"Corion, prepare our transfer to the launchpad. Lark and Asher, help Leo suit up. Let's go!"

With the two of them on either side of me, helping me into the thirty-pound, blue-gray pressure suit and its attached survival backpack, it hits me with dizzying force: *This is real. This is actually happening.*

Lark and Asher help me lock in my communications cap and full pressure helmet as I step into heavy black space boots and slip on pressure gloves. Then, after Greta's looked me over and checked my oxygen levels—we're off.

We march out the lab doors, with Greta, Asher, and Lark surrounding me like I'm a prizefighter and they're my ring crew. Corion is waiting in the front seat of a self-driving, six-tire All-Terrain Mobility Platform, a modern version of the open-air army vehicles you'd find in a war zone. It takes all four pairs of hands to help me climb up to my seat in the gathering storm, my heavyweight gear making each movement intense with effort. And then the wheels start skidding up the path from Greta's lair, the wind whipping us through curves as we traverse the one-mile stretch of canopied trees to reach the main attraction: her private lake, with its own rocket barge. There, like a beacon beneath the clouds, is the *WagnerOne*: a sleek, compact, and mighty rocket ship built for another world.

"Holy . . . wow." Asher whistles under his breath. "Can you believe this, dude?"

"No." I shake my head in disbelief. *If my parents and Angelica could see me now . . .*

Greta leads me inside to the flight deck and cockpit, which looks like a shrunken replica of the *Pontus* flight capsule, while another hatch opens into a small, one-room cabin with a bolted-down single bed, kitchenette, shower, and toilet. It is stark and minimalist, with no added comforts like on the *Pontus*, but I know why. The viability of the *WagnerOne* lies in its weight and speed. The smaller and faster we can be, the quicker we'll catch up to the *Pontus*, and the less effect our added weight will have on their trajectory when the two of us—*incrociamo le dita*, fingers crossed!—manage to dock.

Heading back to the flight deck, I nearly jump out of my skin when a gray square console that I thought was part of the cockpit starts *walking* toward us.

"Commander Danieli," the square . . . thing says. A metallic light darts from its surface as it speaks. "I look forward to serving you."

I spin around to face Greta.

"A robot? I'm flying with an AI?"

"His name is Kitt," Greta replies. "We didn't have the room for a humanoid, but Kitt is a very capable bot who will be able to assist you with day-to-day tasks aboard the ship."

I throw my arms around her, feeling a rush of gratitude. Greta looks slightly bewildered at first, but then she gives me a tentative hug in return. When she steps back, I'm surprised to see a glint of tears behind her glasses. I look away, knowing she wouldn't want me to notice.

"I thought I was going to be completely alone up there," I say. "I can't believe you didn't tell me about Kitt sooner!"

"Well, I didn't want you to get lax in your training," she says with a wry smile. "Also, Kitt has only been programmed with enough memory and battery life to last until Europa. After that, he'll be deactivated, so you can't get too attached."

"Oh." I pause. "Well, still. Thank you."

She nods. "Are you ready to say your good-byes?"

"Wait." I lower my voice, looking outside the capsule door to where Asher and Lark are standing. "What's going to happen to them after this? Will you keep them safe?"

"You have my word," she promises. "They will both be employed by Wagner Enterprises for as long as they'd like, with their choice of lodgings and my private security detail looking after them as well."

I release my breath.

"Okay. And there's—there's one other thing I need you to do for me."

Greta raises an eyebrow.

"What's that?"

"Find Naomi Ardalan's brother and parents. Keep an eye on them, make sure they're okay. And if there's somewhere else where they can be safer from all the California floods, with better care for her brother—make that happen for them, please." I give her a slight smile. "You could say it's my last wish."

"Done," Greta agrees. She glances up at the thundering sky. "Ready?"

I nod and step out of the spaceship to see Lark and Asher one last time. It's a memory frozen in my mind, to keep with me for the rest of my life: hugging my only friends left on Earth, the people who saved me from the bleakest future.

"Thank you both, for everything. I'll never forget this. And I'm going to make you guys proud up there."

"Love you, brother." Asher thumps my back as we hug good-bye, his expression bittersweet. "Tell the stars hello from me."

Lark squeezes my hand.

"You're going to be amazing. Good luck up there." And then she whispers in my ear, "Say hi to *Naomi* for me."

"I can't wait to." I smile at the thought.

Greta clears her throat beside me.

"It's time." She meets my eyes, and I can tell she's struggling to keep her emotions at bay. "I don't know if I've said it yet, but—thank you. For being brave enough to take a chance, and for believing in something others might dismiss as the wild ideas of an old, mad scientist."

"You're not that old," I say, trying to keep the mood light so I don't break down.

"And for giving me a purpose again." Her voice is barely audible through the wind, but I know I heard her right. "You sometimes remind me of someone. . . . He would have done well at this. I know you will, too."

At the mention of her son, a chill runs through me. I'm retracing Johannes's steps—hugging Greta good-bye, walking into the spacecraft, preparing for liftoff. But it can't be the same outcome this time . . . can it?

"Thank you," I mumble. "Let's—let's do this."

I watch her walk away to join Asher and Lark, and I give the three of them a final wave. And then, swallowing the lump in my throat, I turn and enter the spacecraft alone.

I strap into my reclined launch seat, going through all

the motions Asher taught me on the piloting touch screen, while trying to ignore the slamming of my heart against my rib cage. The floor beneath me rumbles, the sky outside turning a fiery orange as Greta lights a series of massive wooden sticks, setting them ablaze in quick succession, and the engines ignite. The countdown echoes in my ears from the cabin speakers, and I close my eyes, bracing myself for—

"T-minus one. And . . . LIFTOFF!"

Maybe if we'd left one minute sooner, or if the tornado had struck one minute later, I could have been free of its path entirely. But the second the rocket shoots into the air, I feel the wind's pummeling force, threatening to suck the *WagnerOne* into its vortex. The ship's walls shudder around me, my speed starts to waver, and I watch in horror as the numbers flickering on-screen take a sharp dive. As quickly as my journey began, it's ending. I can feel the storm lashing at the spacecraft, the wind shear yanking us off course; I can already see the crash-landing on Earth to come—

"LEO!" Greta's voice shouts into my headset. "Increase your escape velocity. You can beat this!"

With my hands shaking in their gloves, I quickly work the flight controls, accelerating and swerving and adjusting my trajectory, until at last gravity falls away. The last thing I see is a flash of light—

—and then everything turns black.

PART TWO

MARS

Message Origin: EARTH—United States—
S. California
Message Recipient: *PONTUS* Spacecraft—
Earth-Mars Transit
Attn: ARDALAN, NAOMI
[Message Status: Received—Encrypted]

Hey, Sis.

Last night started out almost like old times at our house, and I mean OLD times, before half of LA flooded and we started living under rations. Dad grilled beef kabobs and Mom cooked her famous Persian rice with cherries, and it was like I was eleven again. At least, that's how long ago it seems since we last ate anything as delicious as kabob or cherry rice. But then, when we were settled in at the couch, there was this gaping, empty space. And when we turned on the TV, instead of catching up on one of our shows or picking a movie to watch, it was *you* on the screen.

I can't explain what a weird feeling it was, to go from a scene that felt so nostalgic, like you could have been sitting right there next to me, to getting hit in the face with the reminder that you're actually in SPACE. Most of the time I think I do a decent job of being strong and cool about all of this, but sometimes it's just . . . a lot. And sometimes the only thing that helps is running up to your room, standing in the middle of your old stuff, and pretending I still have a sister and best friend on Earth.

Anyway . . . Your livestreaming event for the *Final Six* docuseries was the reason Mom and Dad decided to spring for last night's epic dinner, so I gotta thank you for that! In all seriousness, it was *really* good to see you. I wish we got to talk more—it's crazy how they micromanage your time up there—but I know I should just be grateful the technology even exists for us to communicate from hundreds of millions of miles away.

I was thinking about how when we were little, every time we heard of another hurricane or tsunami sending a different city underwater, we'd look at each other and say, "We're living in the future." We meant it in the darkest sense then, but now that you're up in space, changing the world (I mean the universe!), you've redefined what living in the future means, and turned it into a positive. And that is pretty freaking cool.

Speaking of cool . . . I got your encrypted attachment the other night, about your discovery (!!) and I'm attaching some research of my own for you here. Basically, I'm working on a list of Earth organisms that match some of the characteristics you described—that way we can get at least a vague idea of what to expect on Europa. (And yes, I know I said "we," LOL. The truth is, it helps a lot to feel involved in some small way.)

Anyway, something struck me as interesting: I looked up the physiological traits you mentioned, and the same few living creatures came up—but they were all from *prehistoric Earth*. So that tells us something. I leave it up to you, sister-genius, to figure out what.

I'll write you more tomorrow, and Mom and Dad asked me to remind you to send more video messages— we're all missing you big-time.

Love ya,
Sam

TEN

NAOMI

I STAND IN FRONT OF THE SQUARE PLASTIC SMIDGE OF MIR-
ror above my bathroom sink, checking my reflection half an
hour before the landmark Earth-to-Deep Space press conference that will broadcast us live to hundreds of millions in
a special live episode of the *Final Six* docuseries. It's only the
second time astronauts have ever video-chatted with Earth
from this great a distance—nearly halfway to Mars—and I
try not to think about what happened to the last crew as I
run a brush through my hair.

Dr. Takumi told us that more than half of Earth's population is expected to tune in today. I can barely wrap my
head around that staggering a number, but the thought of
my family watching—and maybe, hopefully, Leo—is what

gives me focus. My feelings about the mission may waver, but my desire to make them proud is constant.

"Naomi." A clipped, mechanical voice echoes outside my door, and my back stiffens. *Cyb.* "We're waiting for you."

So far on the ship, there's been a clear divide between the AIs and the human crew. Aside from the first day, Cyb and Tera haven't made a single appearance at our Astronauts' Residence, while only Jian has gone back to the command module where the robots are stationed and where Cyb runs the cockpit. So it's a jolt of surprise when I hear his voice. If Cyb is joining us, this must be more important than I thought.

I slide open my door, stepping out alongside Minka as she exits her room next to mine. The others are lined up by the elevator pod, all of us dressed in our matching *Mission: Europa* uniform shirts per Dr. Takumi and the general's instructions, though a couple of my teammates managed to dress it up even with the limited fashion choices aboard the *Pontus*. Minka pairs the shirt with an asymmetrical skirt over black tights—two items it would have never even occurred to me to pack—while Sydney has on a pair of black jeans with strategic holes at the knees, a throwback to last century's favorite trend. Meanwhile, I'm keeping it simple in my favorite old pair of plain dark blue denim, and it hits me with a sharp pang when I last wore these—the weekend before I left home.

Just then, I notice Tera shuffling forward next to Cyb, a stack of familiar-looking jackets in her mechanical arms. As soon as Minka and I join the group, she begins handing them out to each of us. I'm expecting the usual ice-blue bomber jackets with our mission patch and insignia, but this time there's something else right underneath: an over-size logo at the chest, announcing in bold letters: *Brought to you by ACS Sportswear!*

"What's this about?" I ask Tera, pointing at the logo.

"Our mission's new corporate sponsor," she answers. "All-Climate-Safe Sportswear. Dr. Takumi has instructed me to make sure one of you mentions them live on camera."

I turn to Sydney and Dev next to me, and the three of us exchange bewildered glances.

"Since when do we have sponsors?" I press. "That seems really . . . odd." We're supposed to be colonizing another world and saving humanity from theirs—shilling products hardly fits with either agenda.

"Earth's declining population means declining tax dol-lars, so sponsorship provides a significant source of our mission funding." Tera's voice becomes more monotone than usual as she recites some kind of memorized speech. "Thanks in part to ACS Sportswear, we are able to travel farther than anyone in the history of humankind, in lodg-ings that are as comfortable as they are state-of-the-art. ACS Sportswear is a generous supporter of both Interna-tional Space Training Camp and its brilliant leader, Dr. Ren Takumi and—"

"That's enough, Tera." Cyb's voice cuts through the room, halting the backup robot midsentence. Her mechan-ical mouth snaps shut and her eyes—round blue camera lenses—blink straight ahead as she waits for her superior's next command.

"I believe Tera got a little *confused*." Cyb says the word as derisively as it's possible for a robot to sound, and I find myself suddenly curious about the happenings in the command module. "She took Naomi's question as a prompt to read the prepared statement that one of you will be making on camera about ACS. No need to say the last line, though. Instead, we'd like you to say something to the audience about how ACS Sportswear provides the most durable, weatherproof outerwear to shield their bodies during extreme storms."

"Um. What?"

Jian's mortified expression speaks for the rest of us. The idea of sitting in front of the camera in our billion-dollar spaceship, far removed from the endless spate of hurricanes, floods, and fires on Earth, and using the videoconference to sell outerwear for said natural disasters is revolting. So of course, the one person who volunteers is Beckett Wolfe.

"I'll do it." He shrugs.

"Good. Now let's get into camera position downstairs."

Cyb lumbers toward the elevator pod and the rest of us follow, with me and Dev and Sydney lagging a few paces behind.

"This is going to be embarrassing," Dev says, cringing at Beckett's back.

"I'm getting the idea that this *videoconference* might be just a publicity stunt to make money," I whisper. And then I remember the last line of Tera's awkward speech, the moment Cyb interrupted: *"ACS Sportswear is a generous supporter of both International Space Training Camp and its brilliant leader . . ."*

"He's making money off of us," I blurt out under my breath. "Not just a government salary, but he's taking some of the sponsorship money, too."

And suddenly I know how today is going to go. The anticipated landmark videoconference with Earth is really an excuse to sell more products for ACS, so that they in turn line Dr. Takumi's pockets.

"No wonder he never really cared about the risks and wanted to keep the mission going at all costs." I grit my teeth. "We're his meal ticket."

"I wouldn't go that far." Dev looks taken aback by my mini-tirade and Sydney jabs her elbow into my side, a reminder to cool it in front of him. Dev doesn't know what I discovered at space camp or here in the lab with Sydney; he doesn't know anything about what Dr. Takumi is hiding.

But it's only a matter of time before everything comes to light.

"You three! Get moving."

Cyb's voice makes me jump, my face turning bright red. Did he hear me? But no, the robots are too far ahead. We pick up the pace and meet the rest of our crew in the elevator pod, all of us silent as we swoop from the fourth floor down to the first.

I'd been tasked with setting up the Communications Bay ahead of time, so the main cinema screen is already unfurled and blinking with a countdown clock when we arrive, while two larger cameras are positioned in front of our six chairs. We take our seats in alphabetical order, me at one end and Beckett at the other, with a robot on either side. Thankfully, I have the less intense, slightly bumbling one of the two robots next to me.

Just before the countdown clock hits the two-minute mark, the screen flickers to life, with Dr. Takumi and General Sokolov filling the frame. I shift uncomfortably in my seat. What lines are they planning to feed us now?

"Good afternoon, astronauts and AIs," Dr. Takumi greets us. His deep voice manages to be as resonant through the screen as it is in person. "We'll be going live in just a few moments. You'll be looking at a split screen of the five countries you represent, with a different news anchor stationed at each location. Select audience members have been chosen to ask you questions, so we'll have a short Q and A, and the general and I will make some remarks as well. There will be two commercial breaks, at which point you will give the testimonial for ACS Sportswear, which I assume the robots briefed you on?"

"Roger that," Beckett calls out. "I'm on it."

I try not to roll my eyes.

"All right, then. We're going live in three . . . two . . ."

I hear my mom's voice in my head ("Don't slouch, *azizam*"), and I sit up a little straighter, just for her.

"One."

And then the screen transforms, bursting with color. I stare hungrily, soaking in the vision of everything I miss: the ancient trees and dirt roads, the sound of whipping wind and voices and laughter, the crowds of people, and yes, even the water, the rain and overflowing oceans. I miss it all with a fierceness that makes my eyes sting and my stomach ache.

The split screen gives us a wealth of Earth visuals, and I drink in each of the five scenes: a faded gold temple, standing on pillars above rising water in India; a terraced, sloping green field in China; the front facade of a railway hotel in Canada; a giant staircase leading from the sea to a city square in Ukraine; and the sprawling, elevated campus of Houston's Johnson Space Center, home of Mission Control and our Space Training Camp. These surviving landmarks are a reminder of all the beauty that's left on Earth, even amid the destruction, and I feel a stab of regret that all the resources we're pouring into finding a new home aren't going toward saving the one that's been there for us all this time.

Every location on-screen is filled with hordes of locals who go wild when they see us on their end, shrieking and cheering, some even *crying*, as if we invented music or something else worthy of this kind of adulation. Some are holding up signs with messages and slogans bearing our names, and my heart jumps as I catch one written to me in Farsi.

"Godspeed, Naomi."

I look to see who is holding the sign, and find a girl of

about nine or ten. She looks just like me at that age, with her wide, dark eyes, unruly hair, and those thick eyebrows that she'll probably have to wait a few more years before she's allowed to tweeze. The girl's expression brims with hope, with admiration, and I feel a wave of emotion at the sight. I try to catch her eye through the screen, and I mouth *Thank you*. As much as I ache for home, at least I know that my being here is doing a bit of good.

"Greetings, all!" Dr. Takumi booms. "We are now live, from Earth to deep space. Everyone, say hello from your respective corner of the world—or, in the case of the Final Six, the universe!"

A chorus of hellos follows in multiple languages, and I smile at the camera, attempting to make eye contact with the crowds on all five sections of the screen.

"We're going to kick things off here in Houston, home of the space program," Dr. Takumi continues. "Now, General Sokolov, I believe you've selected some members of our audience here to ask the Final Six their pressing questions?"

"That's right." The general steps into frame. "First, we have twelve-year-old Cooper Grace, the youngest in a family that's been residing in Houston for four generations now. Tell us, Cooper, what is your question for the Final Six?"

We all smile at the boy as he tentatively approaches the general, his cheeks bright red.

"W-what do you do all day on the spaceship?" he whispers into the microphone.

"A very good question," the general tells him before

turning back to face us through the screen. "Why don't you each introduce yourselves and talk a bit about your different roles? Jian, let's start with you."

"Ah. Okay." Jian clears his throat. "My name is Jian Soo, from Tianjin, China—" He pauses, grinning at the roar of excitement emanating from the China segment of the screen. "I'm the copilot, which means I assist Cyb, our genius AI pilot over here, with flight duties and navigation. I go into the command module once a day to monitor our trajectory and progress, and take care of anything that needs a human touch." He looks at Cyb with a sheepish smile. "Most of the credit belongs to him so far, but I'll have more to do when the Mars maneuver and Europa landing are finally here."

"Oh, yes you will," the general chimes in. "Minka?"

"I'm Minka Palladin from Odessa, Ukraine. Those steps you're standing on—they're less than a mile from my home." There's a slight wobble in her voice that I've never heard before as she stares at the screen. "I—I'm the mission science officer. My job on the *Pontus* is to carry out different lab experiments that Dr. Takumi or General Sokolov assigns me, like testing different methods of creating oxygen, food, and other essentials that we'll need when we get to Europa. Once we land, I'll also serve as mission chemist."

We continue with Dev, whose role as lieutenant commander includes leading all EVA/spacewalk operations and facilitating the docking of our ship with the Mars supply vessel, and Sydney, who speaks haltingly about administering the RRB, focusing more of her job description on all the medical care she'll eventually be responsible for. And then it's Beckett's turn. He gives the camera a casual wave and his trademark cocky grin before introducing himself, waiting a beat for the impressed crowd murmurs that always accompany his famous last name.

"I'm the underwater specialist, which means I'm in charge of all things related to Europa's ocean and our terraforming efforts on the ground," he says. I stare at the floor to hide the disdain surely written across my face. *It was never supposed to be you.*

"Once we land, I'll be the one making the dangerous treks below the ice, driving the submersible back and forth in a foreign ocean as we explore and develop the new world." He gazes into the camera with an expression so solemn, it would make me laugh out loud if I wasn't so annoyed. "It's a serious responsibility, but my swimming career has prepared me well."

I stifle a snort. I wouldn't really call captaining his high school swim team a "career," but ooookay. Just as I'm gearing up to answer the question myself, Cooper, who seems to have dropped his shyness by now, asks Beckett a follow-up question.

"Then you must be so bored on the spaceship, with no ocean yet and nothing to do!" he says, his round eyes widening. "Do you just . . . hang out and watch TV all day?"

The audience on-screen laughs at the boy's comment, while Beckett visibly bristles.

"Hardly," he says evenly. "I have my own highly

important tasks on the ship as well."

"Like what?"

I glance over at Beckett, and I can see it in his face—there's no way he's letting a twelve-year-old show him up in front of the world on live TV.

"Like being the one astronaut with access to the ship's 3D-printing lab, where we're developing next-level tools for surviving Europa. If you think you've seen high-tech before, well. Just wait till you see this."

Beckett raises an eyebrow, practically daring the audience not to be impressed. He has nothing to worry about there. The faces on-screen light up in awe, friends and family members turning to each other with murmurs of "Whoa" and "So cool."

My first instinct is that Beckett is lying, of course. We don't *have* a 3D-printing lab on the *Pontus*. That's not the kind of thing you fail to notice. But then I catch General Sokolov's frozen expression on-screen. She looks . . . blindsided. Like Beckett let slip something he wasn't supposed to.

"Naomi?" she says, after a beat of silence.

Everyone turns to me now, waiting for me to dive into my job description, but I'm still reeling from Beckett's revelation. What could possibly be happening that would make Dr. Takumi and General Sokolov want to keep the 3D-printing lab a secret from everyone but *Beckett*, of all people? Because, based on the befuddled expressions around me, it seems most of my teammates are just as in the dark as I am. Only Minka remains poker-faced. I wonder if she's heard him boasting about this before.

I manage to give the viewers a semi-coherent rundown of my life as the ship's communications and technology specialist, but I'm only halfway present. *What, exactly, are they making in that lab?*

"Now before we throw it to our next location, we have a surprise for our Americans onboard," Dr. Takumi says. He's performing for the crowd now, not making eye contact with either Beckett or me. "Your families each sent a gift for you, to be opened live on-air during this videoconference. The gifts will be displayed in a place of prominence here at Mission Control, representing you in front of the many employees who are working day and night to keep you safe."

I lean forward, my heartbeat picking up speed. Seeing what my parents and Sam picked for me will be almost like having them there.

"And the first gift is for . . ." One of Dr. Takumi's aides hands him a package. "Naomi. Ready for me to open it?"

I nod quickly, staring at the screen as he tears off the wrapping paper. Dr Takumi lifts the lid from the box and unearths a canvas awash in shades of red, blue, and gold. It's a painting of a woman, rising tall and mighty, her back arched in a warrior pose as she holds a sky-high staff and lifts her face to the heavens. Her jet-black hair is pulled back with a golden diadem of stars, while two towering angel wings extend from the back of her crimson dress.

"The Iranian goddess Anahita," Dr. Takumi reads from a caption carved into the frame of the painting. "Goddess of water, ruler of the stars."

She is magnificent. Everything about her, from her pose to expression, makes me feel proud, strong, capable of anything. I reach out a hand, wishing I could get closer to my gift, close enough to feel the paint under my palm.

"There's something written on the back!" one of the audience members yells excitedly.

Dr. Takumi gives them a scolding glance before turning the canvas over to read, *"For our beloved Naomi: a symbol of the old world and the strength and power you come from, qualities that we know will carry you through your journey into the new. Always remember how loved you are—Mama, Dad, and Sam."*

I blink back tears, but this time, they're not from sadness. I feel them with me. And I know that it's not just qualities like strength that will carry me through the journey to Europa—it's love.

"Thank you," I finally manage to say into the camera. "Mom, Daddy, Sam . . . this means more than you know."

I only wish I had it here, to hang by my bed. I'll have to look up a photo of the painting as soon as the videoconference is over, to save onto my tablet.

"Next up, Beckett!"

Everyone peers forward as Dr. Takumi unwraps a smaller parcel, curious to see the kind of gift coming from the realm of the White House.

"Ah . . . would you look at that." Dr. Takumi lifts a thick black book with silver calligraphy lettering across the spine, the cover decorated in coats of arms. "A first edition copy of *He Who Drew the Sword*, the classic American novel published in 1938!"

I draw in my breath. That is a seriously old relic. I give Beckett a sidelong glance, but he doesn't seem nearly as impressed with the gift as the rest of us. He seems almost frustrated, and I wonder if he was expecting something showier.

"Is there a message with that one, too?" an audience member calls out.

Dr. Takumi carefully flips through the delicate pages and double-checks the parcel, but comes up with nothing.

I think about my family's loving words to me, and I almost feel sorry for Beckett. *Almost*. But the feeling slips away as fast as it came on with the first commercial break. Beckett jumps into salesman mode for the unsuspecting viewers on Earth without a hint of irony, making ACS Sportswear sound like a miracle jacket that will ward off all horrors of climate change. This time, I can't refrain from rolling my eyes, even on live TV.

The videoconference POV location shifts from the United States to India, and I relax back into my seat as Dr. Takumi and General Sokolov fade into the background. Still, I can't shake Beckett's words from earlier. I can't stop wondering about the supposed 3D-printing lab . . . and whether it holds the answer to the secrets that I know the three of them are keeping.

ELEVEN

LEO

I DRIFT IN AND OUT OF CONSCIOUSNESS, CERTAIN I'M IN THE wrong place every time I open my eyes. My lids seem glued shut—it takes too much effort to pry them open, and when I finally do, I can barely see anything through my blurred vision. All I can make out is the hazy form of a console with a large, dark window in front of it. And then there's something gray that's moving, lumbering around me like a big, pesky fly. I reach out, trying to squash it, but my head hits the seat again, my eyes close—and I'm gone.

The next time I wake, it's to the sound of my own screams. I'm falling, my body sliding down in its seat, only there's no ground, no place to land. Something wet and cold presses against my forehead as a strange voice says, "The pain medicine should kick in soon. Your head took a bad hit, but you'll be all right. Can't launch in a tornado without consequences, it seems."

I groan, turn my head away from the voice that I can't see, and the background noise starts to fade. . . .

I have no clue how long it's been when I wake up next, this time with a ringing in my ears. It sounds like an alarm of some kind, and I sit up too fast; the room starts spinning around me. I wait for it to stop, for my equilibrium to return, but it only gets worse, and now I'm whipping forward in my seat, the strap digging into my suit as my stomach plummets.

"Make it stop!" I yell, covering my throbbing head.

"Dr. Wagner, we have a big problem here," the strange voice babbles near me. "We're rolling, and our rate of spin is accelerating fast. I don't know where the malfunction is, but the ship started banking and I can't get control—"

We're pitching forward now, and I let out a strangled scream. *What is happening? Where am I, what is this?*

I look up frantically, and that's when it hits me—I can see again. The haze has cleared. And I'm looking up at a window in the ceiling that shows me nothing but a black, starry sky.

The mission. It comes slamming back to the surface, the details flooding my mind like a movie montage as I remember everything. And just in time, too—because we're in major trouble.

My hand shakes as I swipe my wrist monitor.

"Dr. Wagner, it's Leo. Do you copy? I seem to have sustained some type of injury, but I'm now awake and fairly *alert*—" My last word comes out in a yell as our capsule starts spinning even faster. "What is happening to our ship?"

"Leo, we're running diagnostics on the *WagnerOne* from our end and should have our results momentarily," Greta Wagner answers. She's trying to sound calm, but I hear the breathlessness in her voice, the strain of fear.

I shout as the ship rolls again, tumbling once more, and now I'm not just worried about how fast we're spinning, but the direction. We're moving farther away from the *Pontus*'s trajectory, and if we don't make it—

"It's the maneuvering thruster!" Greta's voice yells in my ear. "Something's wrong with it—a short circuit in the wiring, most likely caused by the impact of the tornado when it came into contact with the ship. Let's start with a reboot. Do you copy?"

My fingers fumble on the control panel until I find the power switch for the maneuvering thrusters, and I quickly turn them off and back on again. But nothing changes—and now we're moving even faster.

"Approaching one revolution per second!" Kitt barks into the speaker. "How can we fix this?"

The tumbling is so violently fast it feels like the force of speed is strong enough to pull the organs from my body. My eyes return to blurring, my head about to hit the chair for the last time, when I hear—

"Turn those off altogether and use the control system thrusters at the front of the ship instead," Greta instructs.

"It's one of the things we practiced just the other day," another voice calls through my headset. *Asher*. "You can do it, Leo."

I can do it. I have to.

I switch off one set of thrusters on the command module and then scan the touch screen, searching for what I need. Finally, I locate the front control system thrusters, which normally shouldn't be activated till landing—yet I have no choice but to use them now. I'm prematurely activating thrusters that aren't supposed to be deployed until landing—the same maneuver that got Greta's son killed on another Wagner ship before this one.

My hand freezes over the row of buttons. I can't decide, can't move. Until I hear Asher yell, "*Now*, Leo! This is all we've got."

Our capsule takes another sideways dive, and I slam my palm onto the button. Relief is on its way—either that, or the end. And it'll be another excruciating few minutes before I know which it's going to be.

TWELVE

NAOMI

AN HOUR BEFORE THE NEXT SCHEDULED ROUND OF RRB injections, Sydney and I huddle up in my room, trying to solve our trickiest equation yet.

"So, Option A," Sydney begins. "We confront Dr. Takumi and General Sokolov with what we know about the RRB, and refuse to administer any more injections until they tell us the full truth about what kind of organism this bacteria really *is*, and what it will do in the long run."

"It is the simplest choice," I say wistfully. "But probably the most flawed. At this point, I don't trust Takumi or the general to tell us the truth about the weather, much less something as secretive as the RRB. So I don't think we could bank on any real answers from them. But more importantly than that, we've seen how the two of them can control the ship from their end. The last thing we want is a retaliation, when we can't fight back."

"Ugh. Yeah." Sydney twists one of her long black curls around her finger, exhaling in frustration. "So what's Option B? Do we even have one?"

"I was thinking we might replace the serum with something else," I suggest. "I can try to think up and replicate some harmless control substance, like a placebo, that would look similar to the RRB on camera. I obviously can't do it in time for tonight, but sometime this week seems doable. No one but us would have to know that it's just a placebo."

"I thought about that too. But then . . . what if we really do need the RRB, as creepy as what's inside it might be?" Sydney's face creases with worry. "What if I stop the injections and we find out our crew can't handle the radiation without them?"

I stare at the sliver of stars through my window, equally stumped.

"We have a few more months before we get close enough to the radiation danger zone, so we could just give the control substance until then," I muse. "In the meantime, I think the key is finding out what *kind* of life is in the RRB—and waiting for us on Europa. You mentioned my notes pointed to some type of . . . sea monster." I shudder. "And I shared the same notes with my brother back home, who pointed out the similarities with prehistoric Earth creatures. So are we talking intelligent life or wild? Is it something we can coexist with or not? If we can find that out before we reach Jupiter orbit, and really know what we're dealing with, that just might save our lives."

"That all sounds right, but . . . how?" Sydney wonders. "You already saw all the data Dot had, right?"

"There is one other thing I can try," I say slowly. "I can send out a signal from our ship to Europa. Whether or not we get any sort of response will tell us a lot."

Sydney nods, and I'm surprised to feel a flicker of excitement. Though I guess it shouldn't be too shocking. I may not have chosen to end up here on the *Pontus*, but there are few things I love as much as having a plan—especially one that allows me to take up the Space Conspirator mantle in the search for life.

"What did you think about Beckett's whole bombshell today?" I ask. "Have you seen anything that could be a 3D-printing lab on the *Pontus*?"

"That's what I was trying to figure out the whole time he was talking. Where would something like that be? Unless . . . was he just bluffing?"

"No . . ." My voice trails off. "I mean, I wouldn't put it past him to lie, but I think this was him actually telling the truth. Maybe saying too much."

Sydney flops backward on my bed, looking as exhausted by all this as I feel.

"What have we gotten ourselves into here?"

"Seriously."

"To think, I just wanted to be a plain old doctor when I

grew up," she gripes. "Now look at me. I'm—I'm in a giant machine flying through outer space, strategizing about *aliens* with a girl who, just three days ago, I thought was probably delusional." She pauses and gives me an apologetic smile. "Sorry about that, by the way."

"It's okay." I can't help but laugh. "Life had other plans, apparently. For all six of us."

"I am glad you're here, though." Sydney sits up to face mer. "You—and Dev—make this a lot less scary."

"Ditto," I tell her. "Speaking of Dev. Are you two . . . a thing?" I give her a mischievous grin, and she tosses a pillow at me.

"No—yes. I don't know. Maybe."

"Well, we've got one Europa 'partnership' squared away then." I wiggle my eyebrows at her and we both start giggling. For a brief moment, the weight of the world drops from our shoulders—and we get to be teenagers again.

I slip down to the Communications Bay after dinner, ready to enact the first step of our plan. Sitting at my touch-screen desk, it hits me—this is the first time where, instead of sliding on headphones and listening for radio signals, I am sending one of my own. It's a move that scientists of the past, the ones I grew up learning about like Stephen Hawking and Elon Musk, would have almost certainly cautioned against. But we're well past the point of caution.

I open the Deep Space Network software on my computer and begin by adjusting one of our low-gain antennas to point away from Earth, toward Europa. After that, the question is—*what* should I send to these hypothetical beings we'll soon be sharing a world with? How do I send a message that manages to convey our presence without announcing ourselves as a threat; that can lead to an answer as to whether or not Europa's life is intelligent?

And then I think of Leo's message to me. As the lyrics and melody to "Caruso" float through my mind, I suddenly know just what kind of signal to send.

My pulse quickens as I open our crew's shared music folder and run a search for my dad's favorite old Radiohead song. As soon as I find it, and that haunting chord progression starts to play—it's like being transported home. I can practically smell Mom's rice cooking; I can feel the fabric of Dad's wool coat as he steps through the front door, and Sam and I rush to meet him.

> "... *In the flood, you'll build an Ark*
> *And sail us to the moon* ..."

The perfect song—that makes for a perfect message.

My fingers fly across the touch-screen keyboard, encoding "Sail to the Moon" into a radio-wave message. And then I hold my breath and beam it across the stars to Europa.

Afterward, I sit with my arms around my knees, doing some quick math in my head to figure out how soon my signal could hit its target. Based on our current distance from Jupiter orbit, I calculate it'll be half an hour at most. A shiver runs down my spine at the reality of it.

I've just attempted to make alien contact—and even if I wanted to, I'll never be able to take it back.

At the sound of whirring from the elevator pod, my head snaps up. The doors glide open, and Beckett Wolfe steps out. I hastily log off of my account on the touch-screen desk, and stand up.

"What are you doing here?" He eyes my desk curiously.

"It's my personal time. What do you care where I spend it?" I retort.

"I'm just looking out for the ship and her crew," Beckett says breezily. "Making sure the usual suspects aren't causing too much trouble." He gives me a pointed look. "As I promised Dr. Takumi and the general I would."

"What do you have on the two of them, anyway?" I demand. "There's no way they'd just hand you so much responsibility and special treatment, unless you had something to hold over their heads."

"Sounds like someone might be a little jealous," Beckett says, his voice dripping with faux-concern. "What, were you the star student back home who's finding it hard to watch someone else be the favorite now?"

"You are so full of it," I hiss. I push past him toward the elevator pod, but Beckett slides in front of it, blocking my path.

"What are you and Sydney whispering so much about lately?"

"We're planning a coup, to overthrow you," I say

sarcastically. "It's called friendship. Now let me through."

Beckett steps back the slightest inch, and I squeeze through toward the elevator. But before I step inside, I call out a question of my own.

"What about you? Off to your not-so-secret 3D-printing lab?"

He stiffens.

"If you think I'm going to tell you about it, you're sadly wrong."

"Why? Saving the details for our next TV appearance?"

He doesn't answer, and I can tell from his expression that I've struck a nerve. Dr. Takumi and the general must have chewed him out after the press conference.

"So what *are* you guys making in there that's so hush-hush? Weapons or something?"

I'm trying to catch him, make him slip like he did before on TV. But this time, he stays quiet. He doesn't flinch—not until I say the word "weapons."

The elevator starts to close, and I wedge my foot in the door to keep it open.

"Come on—one secret for another," I say on a whim, unable to hold back my curiosity. "I'll tell you what me and Sydney were talking about if you show me the 3D lab. We can go right now."

"Thanks, but no thanks," he says dryly. "Some things are none of your business. Besides, I don't think your gossip qualifies as an even trade."

I narrow my eyes at him, feeling my blood start to boil.

"If you think I've ever in my life had *time* for gossip, you're more clueless than I thought."

I let the elevator door slam shut. It was stupid of me to think I could negotiate with him.

I'll just have to find out the truth about the weapons they're building myself.

THIRTEEN

LEO

THE CRINKLE OF STATIC AND THE SOUND OF MUFFLED BREATH-
ing in my earpiece send me hurtling out of my chair in relief.
It's been three days since I had any human contact—three
interminable days of staring out at the dark universe while
time turned in on itself, stretching on forever and threatening to suck me into the void. There was nothing for me
to do but wait, my mind stuck on an endless replay of our
harrowing launch. Greta might have called me brave before
I left, but if I'd known what that first hour would be like,
when our capsule went into an uncontrollable spin—I'm
not sure if I still would have had the guts to go.

It was twenty-seven minutes of roll, at the most excruciating speed you can imagine. According to Greta and Asher,

by minute twenty-nine, I would have been dead. No human organs can survive that many revolutions per second. Their directions saved my life, with only two minutes to spare. It's the inverse of what happened to Johannes, and I can't tell what I feel more of: gratitude or guilt.

After disabling the maneuvering thruster and activating the control system engines instead, we righted our course and, thankfully, it's been smooth flying since. But that doesn't stop the cold brick of fear from filling my chest every time I feel the ship pitch or accelerate—a fear made that much worse when there's no other human to talk to.

Now, finally, it seems I'm getting an answer to the dozens of messages I've been radioing down to Earth. I wait for the person on the other end to speak, jittery with anticipation.

"Leo." It's Lark. Her voice sounds different, muffled. It must be the long distance.

"There you are!" I exclaim. "I've been waiting forever up here. I was starting to think something was wrong."

"I know. I'm sorry. We've been dealing with back-to-back storms since the tornado, plus managing the fallout from the ISTC learning about your launch." She lets out a weary laugh. "Space sounds a lot more chill than home right about now."

"Oh." My stomach tightens with guilt. "Are you guys okay?"

"We will be. It's a good thing Greta has a bang-up security team. Anyway, I have to run, but just wanted to let you know not to worry if it gets quiet on our end. We have a satellite tracking your ship at all times, so even when we're not in direct contact, we'll always be checking on you and making sure everything is running smoothly."

"Um, okay, but why—"

"I'm so sorry, I really do need to run. I'll touch base again as soon as I can, but in the meantime, try to enjoy the calm before the chaos. These couple months before Mars will go by faster than you think!"

With that, the radio receiver turns silent. I stare at it in disbelief. If I didn't know better, I'd think Lark was avoiding me. What was up with that rushed, strange conversation?

I float aimlessly through the capsule trying to calm my spinning mind. When I get close to the cockpit, Kitt's gray square exterior lights up.

"Cabin fever?" the AI guesses. "I should remind you that you have a full hard drive of television shows and movies from Earth loaded onto the touch screens here, if you need—"

"I'm fine," I interrupt.

"Including the new episode of the *Final Six* docuseries," he continues, oblivious to my tone. "It came through this morning in our daily uplink."

I pause. In all the chaos of my sped-up training schedule and launch, I forgot there even was a series about the Final Six. And with Greta warning me not to make any contact with the *Pontus* until we reach Mars orbit, to avoid the ISTC tracking and sabotaging our mission, this is my only way of seeing Naomi.

"Thank you," I tell Kitt, before moving toward the desk. I log onto the touch screen and do a quick search for the *Final Six* docuseries, holding my breath while I wait for it to load.

There they are. The episode opens with two astronauts running alongside each other in the ship's gym, the treadmills beneath their feet transforming to a verdant forest ground, thanks to virtual reality. The camera pans up from their legs, and that's when I see who it is: Jian and *Naomi.* I stare at the screen, taking in her glistening olive skin, the sweep of black hair pulled back from her face, dark brown eyes narrowed in concentration. I swallow hard. As their workout winds down, she leans over to nudge him and murmurs something in his ear that makes him crack up with laughter. His eyes follow Naomi after she hops off the treadmill, the grin still stuck on his face—and that's when I know. Jian Soo has a crush on Naomi.

The scene cuts to Beckett and Dev on a mock training mission, and that's my cue to switch it off. I try to move on, to distract myself with one of my many daily tasks around the ship, but I keep thinking about Jian's expression. Is there any chance she'll start to feel something for him, too? What if by the time I get there, it's too late?

TWO WEEKS LATER . . .

FOURTEEN

"SOMEONE WANTED US CUT OFF AND ISOLATED FROM THE entire world. Why?"

"Not just someone. One of us."

I turn sharply at Dev's reply. Our eyes meet, and I can see my own fear, dread, and suspicion reflected in his.

I push off the handrail, my palms slipping in my haste for escape. The terror has my mind reverting to that of a child, with one illogical thought screaming above the others. *Get away from here, away from him—and get back to the moment before.* If I can just shut the door on the payload bay, maybe I can somehow erase the memory of what we discovered here; maybe I can return to the security of still believing my family is only a video-chat away. I've never bought into magical thinking before, but my desperation has me half convinced that if I can just believe hard enough—then maybe my headset will soon start crackling again with voices from Earth.

Floating to the hatch door in my current state is like treading quicksand. I feel the walls closing in around me as I try to move forward, their shadows sucking the breath from my lungs. The coiled wires running across the floor become claws, reaching out to ensnare me, while the hiss of equipment is like the sound a predator makes just before it strikes. Everywhere I look now, the spacecraft seems different, menacing—like it's coming to life and out for blood.

"Naomi! Watch out!"

I feel hands pushing on my back, and I gasp as my body hurtles forward, right before a heavy round weight barrels past. It's the stray bolt, completing another loop in its never-ending cycle around the module.

"Thanks," I murmur to Dev. Staring at the bolt, and realizing just how close I came to getting all consciousness knocked out of me, lifts me from my trance. Adrenaline overrides my shock and I move at full speed, swinging from one handrail to the next with Dev right behind me, until we reach the hatch door. He cranks it open and we dive into the tunnel, floating side by side through the dark, winding nodes that lead to the Astronauts' Residence. The light from our wrist monitors guides our path, and I swipe at mine until Jian's face pops up on the screen.

"Jian, we're on our way back," I yell into the built-in

mic. "Can you gather the others and meet us in the Communications Bay?"

By the time we get there, we find four tense faces crowded around the hatch opening. Jian catches my eye as we climb out, and his expression freezes. He knows.

"Well?" Minka presses. "What's happening?"

I glance at her, at each of my crewmates, and my heart starts thudding at a sprinter's pace. Who was it? Who could pull off this level of sabotage? Beckett seems like the obvious answer, but as I look at him now, with his usual confident swagger conspicuously missing, I wonder if he is even capable of it. If he is . . . then that means I've underestimated Beckett this entire time.

"We've lost all contact with the ground," I reveal. "Someone—someone destroyed the X-band antenna system, and threw it out the payload door. It's gone."

"What?!"

"But how—"

I turn away from the cries of shock and look up at the dark screens surrounding us. It's hard to believe they were so recently filled with hundreds of faces; that we could speak to five different countries at once like it was nothing. Now, next to dead screens and silent radios, that memory feels like it's been lifted from another life.

"What I want to know is who did this to us. Beckett?" My voice shakes with barely controlled rage. "Do you have something to confess? We all know you're the only one with a real motive here."

"What?" he sputters. "What are you talking about?"

"I didn't forget what the general said. 'One of you will assume the leadership role in our place, whenever Dr. Takumi and I are unreachable.'" I meet his eyes, my skin turning hot with fury. "They made you de facto leader, and you were all too eager to make that position permanent. Right?"

"Sonofa—" Jian lunges toward him, but Dev yanks him back.

"Wait a second! We don't know for sure that it was even him."

"It wasn't," Beckett insists. "I swear. Just think about it—without a connection to Houston, there's no one to enforce me as leader anyway. That so-called motive makes zero sense." His eyes sharpen in my direction. "Naomi, on the other hand . . . you've already sabotaged us once, with what you did to Dot. I've seen you break the rules more times than I can count. And, hello, communications and tech specialist?" His voice lowers to a tone that makes my skin crawl. "The antenna is your domain. No one else's."

I shake my head in disbelief.

"You really have lost your mind if you think you can pin this on me."

But as I glance back at my teammates, I realize with a jolt that no one is rushing to my defense just yet. They look from me to Beckett warily, until Sydney finally speaks up.

"No. Naomi wouldn't do this. She has a family back home."

"Exactly." My voice breaks, and I wrap my arms around my chest. "I can't lose them. I can't let them think they've lost me."

"So then, who did do it?" Minka demands. Of course, no one says a word. "And what are we supposed to do now?"

We fall into silence, broken only by the sound of Dev's pacing footsteps. And then I jump up at a flash of inspiration.

"The robots have their own implanted comm systems that should work independently of our antenna. It won't be anything like the on-demand connection we had with Earth before . . . but we can still send and receive messages to Houston!"

I race back to the hatch door, not bothering to wait for a reply. Hope is flooding through my chest, and all I can think about is getting to the command module, to Cyb. I can hear the others following behind me, and someone's foot clocks me in the shoulder as we transition to zero gravity. The six of us move through the air in a pack, pushing off hand- and footholds to gain speed as the different capsules of our ship pass in a blur. And then we reach the hatch door with a navigation symbol painted across its face—the command module.

Jian pulls the door open and we float inside, returning to the blinking lights of the cockpit and the vast expanse of black through its cupola windows. We find the robots in their usual positions, with Cyb in the pilot's seat and Tera standing at her post against the wall, her neon-blue eyes raised to the ceiling, where a navigational map plays like a movie on the screen above. There is something almost jarring about the air of calm in here, in the midst of our mission emergency. It's a stark reminder that while Cyb and Tera may have been built to imitate humans—there is nothing human about them.

Cyb's head swivels around to face us.

"What is this about?"

"Naomi found the source of the signal failure," Jian replies, glancing at me to continue.

"The X-band antenna is destroyed. But I think there's still hope for ground communication through you and Tera."

I hear a click as Tera turns her head from the ceiling, joining Cyb in staring at me.

"I don't understand," Cyb says after a pause.

"I'll explain more later, but what's urgent right now is that we need to use your AIOS software to try regaining contact with Dr. Takumi and the general." I step up to the cockpit, eyeing the sliding metal plates on Cyb's torso. "Please."

The robot rises from his seat, and I watch, heart in my throat, as the metal plates slide apart to reveal a rectangular touch screen. He moves his mechanical fingers across the screen, performing a swift series of taps until he reaches the CALL screen. But the short list of contacts—I. SOKOLOV, R. TAKUMI, and HOUSTON MCC—appears in red italics, with a warning symbol next to each name. I have a sinking feeling before Cyb even attempts the first call.

"What's the problem?" Sydney frets over my shoulder after a few minutes of silence.

"I don't—"

My voice cuts off as the message flashes across Cyb's screen. He wasn't programmed for failure, but there it is.

NO SIGNAL—NO CONNECTION FOUND.

"This isn't happening." Jian crumples into his copilot chair, his face ashen.

"They must have been using our antenna as a communications relay. And without it . . ." My voice drops. "I'm going to be sick."

It's every astronaut's worst nightmare—and it's happening to us.

It only takes minutes for our carefully constructed life on the *Pontus* to fall apart. Without contact, there's no agenda to follow or tasks to complete, there's nothing to do, nowhere to be. All we have left is the long, empty stretch of time ahead, as bleak as the dark void outside our ship. I try telling myself that it could be worse, that at least I'm not alone in this. But it's not exactly comforting to be around my crewmates when I know one of them is responsible. How am I supposed to sleep at night, knowing there's someone just steps away from my room who is clearly out to hurt us? I'm still pretty convinced the culprit is Beckett Wolfe—but as the day wears on, my certainty starts to waver. Maybe it's the change in his demeanor since we lost contact that has me looking at the rest of the crew through a new, suspicious lens. His face has gone pale, his expression like an actor who's forgotten all their lines onstage—a mix of shock and panic that's hard to fake. But if Beckett wasn't the one to destroy the antenna . . . then who?

Back at the Astronauts' Residence, the six of us huddle for an emergency meeting in the living room. I study the five faces around me, waiting for a mask to slip, but the culprit plays their part too well. Then again, he's grown up in a house of politicians. Maybe he learned how to pretend from the best of them.

"What happens now?" Dev asks, his voice barely above a whisper. "No one prepared us for this scenario. . . ."

"We—we could go back," Sydney suggests, her eyes lighting up at the thought. "We could go back to Earth orbit and dock with the ISS. They have all the equipment to build us a new antenna, or even a whole new comm system, and they can patch us in with Mission Control right away—"

"Who would tear us to shreds for giving up on the mission," Jian interrupts. "Everyone on Earth would."

"How is it giving up?" Sydney argues. "It's just taking a pause to fix what's broken. That's all."

"Because turning around could cost us the entire thing," I remind her. It hurts to say the words out loud—I wish I could indulge in her fantasy of going home, even for a minute—but I can't deny the truth. "Delaying our trip to Mars means we miss the target alignment window, which tacks on an extra six months to our trip. And there's no way the supply ship will last that long in orbit with its fuel leak."

Jian nods. "If we go back, we're making a definite choice—choosing ourselves over the mission."

We sit in uncomfortable silence until Minka murmurs, "I wish we could."

"Yeah, well, we can't," Beckett says curtly. "I think we're all in agreement here that deserting isn't an option?"

I grit my teeth. It kills me to go along with anything Beckett has to say—especially when we're talking about the difference between returning to my family now, and never seeing them again. But this is bigger than me, bigger than us. I have no choice but to do the right thing.

"So," Beckett continues, when no one contradicts him, "we're just going to have to find a way to make this work—to get through our days in space without any help from the ground. The Mars supply ship has all the pieces we need to set up an advanced comm system once we land on Europa, so it's just a matter of time before we're in contact with everyone again."

"You mean *if* we land," Sydney corrects him. "Our success odds just took a huge nosedive, now that we don't have any guidance from Mission Control."

"We have the robots, though," Jian points out, looking a bit more hopeful than before. "And the *Pontus* is flying a preprogrammed trajectory, so we don't need Mission Control's help there, either. When you think about it, the AIs and our flight software are way more crucial than whether we have contact with Houston."

"We're going to need to get used to only having each other to count on now," I say grimly. "So it sure would be nice if the person here who did this to us would speak up and confess already. That way we can all know who the culprit is, and not have to spend the rest of this journey doubting and second-guessing the other five."

My eyes fall on Beckett as I speak, and he shoots me a look of contempt.

"Yes, Naomi. I want the answer to that question as much as you do."

FIFTEEN

LEO

AN ENTIRE WEEK GOES BY WITHOUT A WORD. I CAN FEEL THE
isolation starting to change me, turning my insides as rag-
ged as I'm sure I look right now, after these restless days and
insomniac nights. My mind is running on a fearful loop,
wondering what could possibly be important enough to
keep Greta, Lark, *and* Asher from communicating, while at
the same time imagining the different scenarios that might
be playing out on the *Pontus* right now. Is Jian in the middle
of charming Naomi, and will I show up to find neither of
them wants me there—

"Leo! Are you there?"

Asher. For a second I think I'm hearing things, but then

he calls my name a second time, and I dash over to the radio receiver.

"Of course I'm here," I snap. "Where else would I be but stuck alone in space on this—this *death trap* of a mission that you all promised to help me through, before suddenly abandoning ship—"

"I knew you'd be mad." Asher sighs. "I get it and I'm sorry, but we had no choice. We had to wait until we were sure we were completely alone—that they weren't watching or listening."

"What are you talking about?" I frown at the radio receiver. "Who's 'they'?"

"The dirty cops Dr. Takumi paid off," he says roughly. "They came back, with orders to arrest Greta for kidnapping and to deliver the three of us back to Houston. There were so many more of them this time—" He breaks off, and my stomach seizes with dread.

"Ash? What happened?"

"They found us." His voice lowers to a whisper. "But Greta gave us a chance to run. She created a distraction by sending in her AIs to fight back against the cops, and then she actually jumped into the fray *with* them, even though she knew they didn't stand a chance against all the police ammunition. It was all just a ploy to keep them busy dealing with her, to buy us time to escape the lab and run to the safehouse Greta told us about."

"So—so you're saying they got her?" I ask in dismay. "Greta's in jail?"

He doesn't answer, and in the pause that follows, I realize it's even worse than that. My heart slams against my chest.

"She's gone." Asher's voice breaks. "The paramedics said the bullets killed her on impact. Greta had to have known this would happen if she tried to fight back, but still she did it, for us." He takes a gulp of breath. "She died to keep all three of us—and your mission—alive."

My hands slip off the railing I'm holding, and my body goes drifting. I can hear Asher calling me, but I don't answer. I couldn't speak even if I wanted to. I'm biting down on my lip so hard that I soon taste blood.

My mentor is dead. That larger-than-life force is extinguished.

And I'm on my own.

Message Origin: EARTH—United States—
S. California
Message Recipient: *PONTUS* Spacecraft—
Earth-Mars Transit
Attn: ARDALAN, NAOMI
[Message Status: Delivery Failure]

Dear Sis,

I'm trying hard not to panic, but the truth is, I've never been this effing scared in my life. Not even the night before my first open-heart surgery, and you know that one was bad. Now all I can do to stay sane is to tell myself over and over that the talking heads on TV are all wrong, that none of the grim scenarios they've painted are real. We may not be able to see you or talk to you, but the satellite trackers still show the *Pontus* making progress, keeping to its trajectory. So I don't—won't—believe the rumors that it's just flying ahead on autopilot. I have to believe you're still alive. It's like Mom said, just before she lit every candle in the house and the three of us sat in a circle to pray: she said that we would feel it if you were gone. We're too close to you not to know. So please, please let her be right. Please be alive and safe.

We had one distraction yesterday—a phone call from your old team leader at space camp, Lark! None of us had spoken to her before, and the last I'd heard about her was that she was apparently missing?! So needless to say, the call was a surprise. At first I was afraid she was reaching out to offer premature "condolences," like some of our neighbors have been dumb enough to do. But it turns out she just called to ask about *us*. She wanted to know everything—how comfortable we are in this new apartment, if it's far enough from the rising tides and fault lines, how my heart medication is working, when my last cardiologist appointment was, etc. THEN she told us something absolutely amazing: she's spent the past few months working for none other than Dr. Greta Wagner . . . and if we need anything at all, to just call and Wagner Enterprises will take care of it! I mean, of all the times to not be able to talk to you! I would give anything to hear your reaction to this.

Mom started crying, and then Dad asked what we owe this kindness to. Lark said it was you—that Dr. Wagner heard how special you are from one of your former teammates, and made a promise to take care of the one thing that mattered most to you: our family.

I said, "This sounds like the guy Naomi told us about, the one I've been trying to find. Leonardo Danieli. Do you know where he is?"

Lark got quiet, and when she spoke again, all she said was that she wished she had more to tell us. She had to go right after that, but promised to call again this week. So that's been the bright spot of our days, and Mom even took it as a sign that you are still out there, and looking out for us from all the way in deep space.

I hope she's right. I hope one day soon you'll be reading these messages. And by then, hopefully we will have answers for you about Leo, too.

We love you,

Sam

SIXTEEN

NAOMI

I PACE UP AND DOWN THE COMMUNICATIONS BAY FOR THE fifth day straight, trying to unlock a solution. There has to be some other way to make contact with Earth, even without the X-band comm system. We still have our smaller low-gain antennas, but they only cover a ten-thousand-mile range. So while I can keep listening for signals and sending out my own, it won't do me much good even if I manage to get a response. Anything close enough for us to communicate with now wouldn't be human.

I slump into the nearest desk chair, in front of the heap of radio equipment I just finished rifling through. I don't have a prayer of reaching Earth with any of this gear, but when my eyes fall on the handheld ham radio transceiver,

I pick it up. We had one of these at home, back when Sam and I were elementary school kids going through a radio phase. Dad helped us set up our own station and choose a call sign (KNS2AR), and Sam and I would "deejay" a show every morning called "A.M. with the Ardalans." I smile at the memory, even though it makes me want to cry at the same time.

I hold the radio close and then, on a whim, I switch on the built-in mic.

"Hello—CQ," I whisper. "This is KNS2AR, calling from the *Pontus* en route to Mars. Can you hear me?"

I close my eyes and repeat the words, but there's only silence on the other end. Just as I expected.

I toss the ham radio back onto the desk and resume pacing, my thoughts returning to my mental list of reasons to suspect—or trust—each of my crewmates. Beckett is obviously far outpacing the others in the "Suspect" column, and I'm mulling over the rest when I hear it—a faint, bell-like sound coming from the headphones I almost forgot I'm still wearing. I freeze, my heart stops, as I listen.

There it is again. Six notes, forming a haunting melody. I reach up with trembling hands to raise the volume in my headphones, and the musical phrase plays again, flooding my insides with a dizzying mix of hope and fear.

With a jolt, I remember the signal I sent to Europa days ago, "Sail to the Moon." Is . . . is this our response?

I practically fly to the computer and open the signal-monitoring software, where a blinking green dot waits for me on-screen—a visual of the signal I'm hearing. I double-click, and the screen reloads with a full page of data on the signal. My eyes scan for the only data entry I care about: location.

The signal's coordinates are as far from Europa as from Earth . . . but the scrolling numbers running across the screen show that the signal is moving closer and closer to us.

I jump up, reaching for the intercom button on the wall to broadcast a message throughout the ship.

"Meet me in the Communications Bay now—all five of you."

My crewmates crowd over my shoulder as I turn the speakers up to full volume and cue the computer to play the signal.

"Here it is." I swallow hard. "Sent to our ship from somewhere in deep space."

The six notes echo through the room, their silvery tones sending goose bumps across my skin. The color drains from Minka's face, Dev and Sydney seize hands, Jian takes shallow gulps of breath. But Beckett's reaction is the one that sticks with me. His is different from the others—less surprised, more ominous—and I'm beginning to think this isn't his first time hearing the signal.

"What the—what does it mean?" Dev sputters.

"All I've got so far are the notes: A-F-A-E-G-A. Does anyone here know if that translates to something?" I look straight at Beckett, but he's back to his poker face, his eyes revealing nothing.

"Considering we're all multilingual, if it's not a word in a language any of us knows, then it must be some type of code," Jian says. "But . . . what code uses musical notes?"

"There was one, back in the days of classical music," Minka speaks up. "I learned about it freshman year. Shostakovich would hide ciphered versions of people's names in the notes of some of his main themes, and it was called a musical cryptogram."

I stare at her.

"Any chance they taught you how to decode those ciphers?"

"Hold on," Dev jumps in before Minka has a chance to answer. "You really think an alien species would communicate with us through a code used hundreds of years ago by some niche group on Earth?"

"Technically we don't know *what* sent it to us—but yes. If they're advanced enough to send us a signal, then they're smart enough to know that music is the universal language," I reply, even as the thought of these sophisticated extraterrestrials makes me shudder. "Minka, any idea how to crack this code?"

"I think I can remember." She steps up to the desk, swiping to open a blank page on-screen. Her fingers trace the screen as she scrawls the seven letters of musical notes, with the letters of the alphabet underneath. "The idea with musical cryptograms is that you're spelling a word through sheet music. But since musical notes only use the first seven letters of the alphabet, certain notes correspond to multiple letters.

So the note A doesn't just stand for the letter A, but also H, O, and V—like this."

A B C D E F G

H I J K L M N

O P Q R S T U

V W X Y Z

"So we have to look at the letters under each note and find the combination that makes the most sense."

She steps back from the screen, and we all stare at it, silently unscrambling the letters.

"Okay, so with the notes being A-F-A-E-G-A, that would spell out to . . ." Dev squints. "Amoluv or Ofozua or—"

"*Athena*," I gasp. I reach up with shaking hands, connecting the letters on-screen. "The signal also happens to spell A-T-H-E-N-A."

Minka lets out a cry of shock, and I hear Beckett swear under his breath.

It's coming from Mars.

"Could it be . . . them?" Sydney whispers. "Alive and still out there?"

"Of course not." Beckett shakes his head. "SatCon has been monitoring Mars orbit and tracking the *Athena* crew for years now. Their biomonitors have been dead the entire time, and there's no trace of human life signatures coming from anywhere near the red planet. For all we know, this is just a stray signal and doesn't mean anything."

"So how do you explain what it spells?" I challenge him.

"Coincidence," he replies without missing a beat. "Besides, who's to say you're right and it's not really Amoluv or something else?"

"Because most of the time in science, and in life, the simplest answer is the right one," I tell him. "And *Athena* is the obvious and simple answer."

There's something else that makes me believe, too. It's the look in Beckett's eyes, his eagerness to explain this away, that lets me know he's scared. And that's how I know, in my core—it's *Athena*.

SEVENTEEN

LEO

IT TOOK MARS TO BRING ME BACK TO LIFE.

The weeks after losing Greta passed by in a dark blur, where days ran into nights and nothing ever changed. I moved like a zombie between my bed and the helm of the ship. I tried to avoid letting myself think or feel too much, but when emotions did creep in, they were like an avalanche of regret. *I never should have done this.*

If I'd just said no to Greta's proposition from the beginning, she would be alive today. Lark and Asher would be safe and free. But instead, I'm alone in an environment that's waiting for the opportunity to kill me—and dragging down my friends on Earth along the way.

I soon stopped keeping track of the days or believing we'd actually get there; I let the ship run on autopilot, with Kitt monitoring our progress. Maybe a part of me even stopped caring. But that changed when I saw the light in the dark—a flash of red in the distance.

"Oh my God."

I gasp for air, convinced my eyes are deceiving me. My legs feel like jelly as I move forward, pressing my hands to the window glass. There it is—

—the flash of red. The beating heart I was searching for.

"We're almost there." My voice comes out like a whisper, and I try again. "Lark, Asher, it a—appears we're approaching Mars orbit. Do you copy?"

The words sound too incredible to be real, like lines from a movie. I whirl around, turning to Kitt and impulsively throwing my arms around him in celebration.

"You hear that, Kitt? We made it!"

The AI emits a *cluck-cluck* sound that I suspect is his version of laughing.

"We have certainly been through a lot these couple of months, Commander."

"Yeah." My smile fades. "Starting with everything we lost. But if Greta's plan works . . ." *Then it could all be worth it*.

It would be the greatest relief of my life, joining up with the *Pontus* and no longer having to navigate all of this alone. I know how lucky I am to have Kitt—I would have gone stir-crazy weeks ago without him—but each time I plug him into his charging pod at night, I'm reminded that he's not real, not in the way of Naomi or Greta. And, as I've learned these past two months, there is nothing so lonely or disorienting as being the only human being for millions of miles.

Our capsule spirals forward, and I can see the red planet better now, looming closer. I let out a whoop of adrenaline, my body thrumming with equal parts excitement and terror. Because this is it—the moment of no return. Either I successfully achieve the rendezvous and docking with the *Pontus* and the Mars supply ship, or I am doomed to flounder in space until I die. Not exactly low pressure.

"Okay, Leo, it's time to begin Mars Orbit Insertion," Lark directs me through my headset. Even she is starting to sound on the edge of her seat.

I nod and, entering the commands on the touch screen, I fire the ship's rockets, slowing my speed to match Mars's orbit. The action brings me back to the day Naomi and I completed a simulation of this very event, the same day I kissed her for the first time—and I am suddenly dizzy at the nearness of her.

This isn't a dream, or a simulation. I am actually looking at Mars. I'm closer to heaven than I've ever been. And I could be just minutes away from seeing Naomi again.

I study the scrolling numbers on the screen in front of me, watching with bated breath as my velocity starts moving closer and closer to that of Mars. And then—with a whoosh that takes my breath away—the *WagnerOne* is sucked into orbit.

My hands shake as I use the Search for Satellite feature on the cockpit's touch screen, watching as, for the first time, it lights up green. *Satellite(s) Found.*

Two green dots blink straight ahead, about a hundred miles apart. The *Pontus* is making headway toward the *Athena* supply ship—and based on the calculations on my Orbital Dynamics screen, I have approximately twenty minutes to catch up. Which means it's finally time to make contact.

I grab the wire transceiver and lean over the microphone, uttering the words I've dreamed about saying for months as I radio the Final Six.

"*Ciao* to my friends on the *Pontus*. This is Leo Danieli, approaching on the *WagnerOne* spacecraft. I've been sent from Earth as reinforcement to your mission, and I'll be close enough to dock in T-minus twenty minutes."

I can barely breathe as I wait for a reply, imagining how Naomi will react, what she will say. But then Kitt reminds me we need to accelerate and I return my focus to the cockpit console, steering us through the air until I am almost in the *Pontus*'s wake.

I continue radioing the Final Six, resending my message every three minutes, but the only response is static. I punch at the wireless, trying to figure out why I'm not receiving a reply—until I hear Kitt shout out, grabbing the joystick in front of me. I follow his gaze just in time to see a flock of laser bullets flying in my direction.

"We're under attack! Lark, Wagner Enterprises, do you

copy? Our ship is under attack!" Kitt barks as I plunge our capsule downward, just missing the strike. But this drop in altitude could cost me everything.

Of all the complicated reactions the Final Six could have had to my arrival, I never would have predicted this. They can't have known it was me, but still . . . what does it say, what does it mean, that their first instinct on seeing a foreign ship isn't to welcome us and ask questions, but to kill? And while I might have survived their attempt, it almost doesn't matter—not now that I've lost alignment with the *Pontus* and am dangerously close to missing the ship altogether.

EIGHTEEN

NAOMI

A WARNING FROM CYB CUTS THROUGH MY DREAMS, HIS VOICE echoing across every room of the *Pontus*.

"ALERT: Suspicious spacecraft sighting. Deploying warning missiles in defense."

What? I struggle to make sense of the words in my groggy state. We're just hours away from our Mars rendezvous, which means we're too far into deep space for there to even *be* another spacecraft. Unless . . . could this have something to do with our last connection to Earth? Did ISTC try sending us a lifeline, only to have our AI mistakenly go into attack mode?

I jump out of bed, not even bothering to change out of my pj's before hightailing it out the door and to the elevator pod. I collide with Sydney along the way, and we make it to the main hatch just as Minka, Beckett, and Dev are climbing through. The five of us move as fast as we can through the winding tunnels and capsules in zero gravity, our panic costing us our coordination as we jab each other with elbows and limbs. Every couple minutes, the ship roars with the sound of hurling weaponry, sending a shudder through the walls and a stab of fear through my chest.

By the time we make it to the command module, the only light I can see through the dark windows is the blinking steel dragonfly in the distance. But I know that ship—it's the same one we've been chasing, the Mars supply vessel.

"What happened?" I demand. "Where's the other spacecraft you saw?"

"Shot down," Cyb says with a mechanical nod. "I've reported the unknown ship to the Deep Space Network. Our sightline is now clear."

"What?" I screech. "Why did you have to attack? What if it was another crew sent by NASA to help us, one with a working connection to Earth—"

"Don't you think Cyb would have recognized if it was an Earth-originating ship?" Beckett gives me a patronizing look. "He's only been programmed with the specific job of protecting us. For all we know, we just dodged a serious alien threat."

"Wait a second." I narrow my eyes. "I thought you didn't believe in aliens, remember? And if that was a real UFO, you really think we were supposed to just shoot it, without making any kind of contact?"

"I followed my training orders," Cyb says calmly. "Co-pilot Soo and I both did as we were taught."

"I didn't really do anything," Jian says uncomfortably. "I barely got a good look at the ship. Cyb is the one who hit the button. . . ." His voice trails off, and then he takes a sharp breath. "But we have a bigger problem."

"What now?" Minka groans.

Jian points to the pilot's touch screen.

"Look at the map. Something's changed. It's now show-ing the supply ship as tracking miles below the orbital plane that our flight navigation software is sending us to. If we stay this course—our ships will bypass each other com-pletely."

My stomach lurches.

"The fuel leak is causing the satellite to drop faster than expected," I realize. "We need to program an orbital inclina-tion change into Cyb's flight nav, starting with recalculating our velocities and position vectors."

The others look at me like I'm speaking a foreign lan-guage. As the resident physics expert here, it falls on me to make sense of the numbers scrolling across the screen, plug them into Kepler's equation, and figure out our new orbital route. Jian offers me his chair and I sink into it, settling in for a night of math ahead.

It takes two attempts to course correct, with me fran-tically scrawling equations across the tablet screen as the *Pontus* flies miles above the Mars supply ship, still treacherously far from its target.

I quickly plug the new trajectory into the flight nav and give Jian back his copilot seat, hovering over his chair as the *Pontus* accelerates and plunges to the correct orbital plane.

The supply ship materializes through the cockpit glass, growing from a light in the dark to a full-fledged satellite looming large. We edge closer and closer to it, and Dev springs into motion, calling out orders for the docking. And then—with a *pop!* and a *click*—the two vessels join together.

"YES!" Dev pumps his fists in the air, throwing his arms around me. Sydney, Jian, and even Minka join him, the five of us celebrating the landmark moment with cheers and a group hug. But something is still nagging at me as I look over at Cyb.

"First Phase Complete," Cyb announces. "Congratulations, crew. Dev, Sydney, and Naomi, it's time to suit up and prepare for your EVA. To confirm, Dev and Sydney will patch up the fuel leak outside the supply ship while Naomi runs diagnostics on the tech inside. Copy?"

"Copy," we answer in unison as Dev spins Sydney around. "Spacewalk time, baby!"

She rubs her hands together with glee. "It's going to be like performing surgery among the stars."

Even though I won't be setting foot outside with the two of them, I still feel shivery with anticipation as Minka and Jian help me into my EVA suit. Dev, Sydney, and I float into the airlock together as the tracking cameras on our wrist monitors flicker on, projecting a live feed of everything we see back to the *Pontus*.

The outer door opens first, and I gasp at the never-ending stretch of black, just waiting to catch us. Dev and Sydney grip hands through their gloves, and I watch their tethers trailing behind them as they step outside, into the void.

After the outer door swings shut behind them, I pull the inner hatch door open and climb out into a dark space capsule, a fraction of the *Pontus*'s size.

"I've entered the *Athena* supply ship," I report into my headset as I feel around for the lights. I spot something glowing in the dark: a spongy amber substance, clinging to the wall outside the airlock. I radio the *Pontus* again.

"Are you guys seeing this? Any idea what it is?"

Minka's voice comes crackling through. "Maybe . . . looks like it could be an exploded food packet?"

I make a face. "Well, that wouldn't bode well for our suppl—"

I break off as my hand finds the light switch, illuminating the room in fluorescent yellow. And then I let out a bloodcurdling scream.

A corpse is floating before me, upside down, its skeletal limbs brushing the ceiling like some kind of horrifying Halloween display. The dead man's body is still clad in a NASA *Athena* space suit, the frayed cloth name tag reading *REMI ANDERS*. A name I know by heart, from my days as a young girl watching every news story I could find on

195

the Mars mission. But there's no recognizing Remi's once-handsome face in the waxy blue mask before me.

I keel over, about to be sick from the sight—and that's when something dark brushes against my helmet. A shout rings through my ears.

"Naomi—in front of you!"

Frozen with dread, it takes every ounce of my courage to look up. That's when I discover Remi Anders wasn't alone.

Four of the five missing *Athena* astronauts are here in the supply ship, their dormant bodies circling on a never-ending loop through the recycled air and microgravity. The same glowing amber substance from the airlock door is smeared across all of their suits.

"Naomi, get out of there and come back to the ship," Jian barks through the headset. "Dev and Sydney, abort spacewalk and return to the *Pontus*. Now."

"But I s-still have to—to get the supplies," I whisper, putting one foot in front of the other as if in a trance.

"The supply vessel is contaminated!" Beckett shouts in my earpiece. "I've seen that stuff before, and we can't risk taking it with us. Let's go!"

"As pilot, I override this command," Cyb interjects. "We cannot leave without procuring the food and supplies needed for the Europa colony."

"But—" I break off at the sound of something familiar, something that sends prickles through my skin. I step forward in spite of my better judgment, following the sound to a radio transmitter—which plays the six-tone musical phrase. A-T-H-E-N-A.

"It was them," I gasp. "The radio-wave message we picked up—it must have been the *Athena* crew's help signal from years ago."

There's a stunned silence on the other end of my earpiece, and then Jian says, "But how could Houston miss something like that?"

"This supply ship wasn't built for human occupancy, so it only has the most basic of comm systems," I say, circling the space. "I don't see any interior cameras, and it looks like they have the bare minimum of radio capabilities—which is why their signal could never reach Earth." My voice breaks. "And why they were never rescued."

"What were they even doing up there?" I hear Minka's voice asking in the background. "They were supposed to be on Martian land, in their Hab—"

"They were running from something," I answer, stopping in my tracks at the glob of amber peeled to the floor—the same substance on the dead astronauts' space suits. Except now it's . . . twitching.

I cover my mouth in horror as the amber starts stretching itself into a new shape, with black stalks sprouting all around it, like the petals of a deformed flower.

"All three of you, get back to the *Pontus* immediately," Jian commands sharply. "Do not touch a thing."

I push my way back toward the airlock, and I'm nearly there when the sound of screaming throws me off track. My hand slips off the railing, my body tumbling backward as

Sydney's voice cries through my earpiece, "Something's out here!"

A skittering sound follows her scream, and I propel myself forward to the small porthole window. I can see Sydney and Dev on the outer module by the open fuel tank, their expressions frozen with terror behind their helmets. And then there's a flash of movement. Sydney staggers back as Dev yells, "It's on her space suit!"

My heart jumps in my throat as I stare out the porthole, scanning for something, anything, they can use.

"The bolts!" I shout. "Grab one of the bolts from the fuel line seal. You can use it to peel that—that thing off."

"And whatever you do, don't bring any trace of it with you," Beckett says, a desperate edge to his voice that I've never heard before.

While Dev reaches for the bolts, I push my way back to the airlock door, leaving the supply ship of horrors behind. I hear the yell in my headset as Dev plunges the bolt into the spongy creature, freeing Sydney from its grasp, and I throw the outer door open.

"Get in here, now!"

A figure swings toward the open door, and I can make out the outline of Dev, pushing Sydney in first. And then, just as he's about to follow her, he lets out a strangled scream.

I crawl toward the door to look and immediately recoil in fear. The amber creature has leaped onto Dev's helmet, covering his eyes. Sydney and I both make a move toward him—but suddenly, without warning, the airlock door slams shut. I pull on the hatch to no avail.

"What did you guys just do?" Sydney shrieks into her headset. "We have to help him—"

"We can't put three astronauts at risk," Cyb speaks up. "I have no choice but to prevent you two from following him. It's what I've been ordered to do."

"But Dev—"

I glance frantically down at the screen on my suit sleeve, and click on "POV—KHANNA." I can see Dev swinging wildly, trying to break free of the creature. And then we hear a sickening crack.

"My helmet—it's breached!" he gasps.

I sink to the floor, praying for this to be a nightmare, for me to wake up back on the *Pontus* with everyone safe and accounted for. But instead, I see that the same bolt that saved Sydney is what struck Dev. And now he has no air to breathe.

"Cover the helmet with your glove!" I yell. "Cyb, open the airlock door! We've got to get him in here before—"

"Not yet—it's still on me—" Dev chokes out.

"He's losing oxygen fast!" Sydney screams. "We have to do something!"

A beeping alarm sounds as the screen on my suit sleeve flashes with Dev's vitals. He only has seconds left to survive without oxygen.

My mind races, formulating a plan—and then I hear the sound of something breaking loose.

I stare at the screen in disbelief as Dev uses his last surge of strength to cut his tether—sending both him and the alien creature floating away from the *Pontus*.

"Th-this is the only way," he whispers.

"What did you do?" Sydney sobs.

"Jian, Cyb, you have to follow him!" I shout.

But it's too late. The low beep of flatlining vitals echoes through our headsets.

Dev Khanna is dead.

NINETEEN

SYDNEY'S WAILS RIP AT MY HEART. I REACH FOR HER, HUG-
ging her through the bulk of our space suits, as my own sobs
break free.

On the other end of our headsets, everything is quiet
except for the sound of someone's repeated whispers of
"No." And then the floor shudders below us as the *Pontus*
undocks from the supply ship—leaving the bodies of the
doomed *Athena* crew, the Martian life, and all the food and
supplies we were counting on to float in space forever.

Sydney and I are forced to spend an interminable thirty
minutes in a second airlock for Decontamination, lying
under machines as our suits are sterilized, unable to speak
or do anything but replay the trauma we just experienced on

a torturous loop. Finally, we're given the all clear to come out, and we emerge in the Astronauts' Residence, where the rest of our team is waiting. But now, instead of the Final Six, we are only five.

We huddle upstairs in the living room, trying to comfort each other in the face of our crushing losses. Sydney is shivering uncontrollably, and Minka finds a blanket to drape around her shoulders.

"We have to turn back now . . . don't we?" Jian asks, voicing what we're all thinking.

I'm surprised to find that the idea doesn't fill me with the relief I expected. But then, this wasn't how I ever wanted it to end—in massive failure, like we went through all this for nothing.

"No." Sydney's voice is quiet but firm. "Dev died for this mission. He died to protect us, so we could continue on to Europa. There is no way we're just turning around and giving up. We didn't do it when we lost contact with Earth, and we're not doing it now."

"She's right," I say, even as my heart twists at the thought of missing the chance to return to my family, to Leo. But I wouldn't be able to live with myself if I let Dev die in vain.

"I don't want to give up either, but what are we supposed to do about food?" Jian asks. "This whole mission was predicated on the assumption that we'd be able to pick up twenty years' worth of supplies from Mars. Now, without that, we only have enough on the *Pontus* for another two years, maybe three if we really stretch our portions."

"How is it better for us to go back to an Earth that doesn't want us there—that spent all this money sending us to a whole other place in the solar system so we could save them?" Beckett counters. "You really think we'll be welcomed with open arms? Besides, we still have more resources on our ship than most people back home. Especially now that . . . well, now that we unfortunately have one less person to feed."

I flinch. It hurts to admit, but Beckett is right.

"We were always planning to start growing food in the solar greenhouse anyway," I point out. "We'll just have to start earlier. The real thing we have to worry about is what we saw today. Extraterrestrials." I give Beckett a sharp look. "You obviously knew about that thing on the supply ship and didn't warn us. So now's your chance to explain—and tell us what you know about Europa."

Beckett shifts uncomfortably in his seat, and I wonder if the expression on his face has something to do with guilt.

"I only knew about the Mars cover-up—that alien life was found on the planet, and its touch was deadly to humans. Dr. Takumi and General Sokolov were the ones who figured it out, and they went to my uncle to report the news before getting NASA involved. But he . . . let's just say, he convinced them not to say anything. My uncle was only halfway through his first term, and he was the one who pushed Congress and NASA to rush the Mars mission, all so we could beat China to it and take the planet as ours. If the American people found out he was responsible for the most dangerous screwup in space-travel history . . ." He raises his eyebrows.

"Anyway, Takumi and Sokolov had good incentive for keeping his secret. He offered them what they always wanted: Europa, and all the glory and riches that would come their way for being at the helm of the mission."

"And your prize for keeping the secret was a spot among the Final Six," I say bitterly. If it hadn't been for Beckett, Leo would be sitting across from me instead.

"Maybe I had an edge, but I still earned my place here," he says evenly. "Same as all of you."

Before I can blow up at him for that obvious lie, Jian quickly changes the subject.

"Why would they tell you, anyway?" he asks. "Who shares that type of confidential info with a kid?"

"Well, the three of them weren't exactly happy when they found me eavesdropping," Beckett says flatly. "I still have the scars from my dad to prove it. But when he found out later what I overheard, he realized the leverage it gave him over his brother." His face darkens. "You're probably getting the picture right about now that being in my family isn't the winning lottery ticket everyone likes to pretend it is. I've lived with humans who are rotten to the core. Why do you think I was so willing to leave Earth behind?"

"Something still doesn't make sense. Obviously, the

Athena proved there's life beyond Earth, and dangerous life at that. Why would any of these people who knew that still insist on the Europa Mission?" I wonder. "Why would President Wolfe still sign off on it? And how in the world could they include a Mars stopover after what they knew was there?"

"Because no one ever thought the supply ship was compromised. Who would have predicted the astronauts would try escaping up to orbit, and that alien life would follow them up to the capsule?" Beckett shakes his head. "And there was nothing to say that Earth would stay ET-free. One of the things I remember Dr. Takumi warning my uncle about was that the missions we'd already taken to and from Mars exposed us to Martian microbes—which could grow into that thing we just saw."

"Panspermia," I murmur.

"Huh?"

"It's the theory that life throughout the universe is distributed through space dust, meteoroids—and spacecraft unknowingly carrying microorganisms," I explain.

"Interesting." Beckett says, more to himself than me. "Dr. Takumi once told my uncle that it was just as likely that the earliest forms of life originated on Europa as on Earth." He pauses. "Maybe that's why our DNA analysis was part of the scouting and selection process.

I stare at him.

"It was?"

Before he can tell us any more, our radio transmitter pings with an unfamiliar signal. The five of us hold a collective breath, our hope charging the capsule with an energy of its own. Is it Earth?

And then Jian shoots upright.

"The other ship—it's back."

TWENTY

LEO

MY PANIC ESCALATES WITH EVERY MINUTE IT TAKES TO regain my velocity and altitude. At this point, each millisecond means the difference between life and death. If I don't manage to catch up to the *Pontus* before the ship slingshots to Jupiter, it's game over. Not just for my mission and reunion with Naomi—but for my life.

My eyes dart between the window shield and the touchscreen panel, where two green targets representing the *Pontus* and the Mars supply ship are drawing closer and closer together. When I see them merge on-screen, I let out an agonized yell. It's over.

There's no way I can make up the speed and distance between us in the short time it'll take for them to patch the fuel leak. The Final Six will slingshot out of Mars orbit, without ever knowing I was here.

"We're done," I whisper to Kitt.

I take my hand off the joystick, letting the ship run on cruise control, not bothering to course correct anymore. My mind starts racing with numbers: how many days' worth of fuel and propulsion our ship has left, how many more hours left to live.

I turn on the Interior Cam to start recording good-bye messages, one for Lark and Asher and another for Naomi. I'm just pressing Record when Kitt's mechanical arm taps my shoulder.

"Commander Danieli. Look."

I glance at the screen, and then I do a double take. For some strange reason, the *Pontus* is undocking from the supply ship. But I don't have time to wonder why they'd make such an antithetical move—I see my split-second chance and slam my hand down on the thruster, going for it.

As we zoom forward at supersonic speed, Kitt reminds me, "We have to make sure they know that it's you, so they don't fire again when they see our ship."

I think quickly. The radio signal didn't work last time— what else can I possibly try?

"Kitt . . . do you know how to beam music to a neighboring spacecraft?"

If Kitt finds the request strange, he doesn't let on. It helps that robots have notoriously good poker faces. Instead, he shows me how to uplink the song I'm thinking of directly to the *Pontus*. And then the strains of "L'Italiano," the song that played as I first stepped off the jet in Houston and met my fellow finalists, starts to echo through the capsule speakers.

With a little luck, right now Naomi is hearing the same thing. . . .

TWENTY-ONE

NAOMI

TIME SLOWS TO A STOP AS THE EXUBERANT MELODY BREAKS through the silent ship, bringing the *Pontus* and its passengers back to life. My first thought is that we've somehow managed to resume transmissions with Earth, that Leo is sending me a message from home—but then I glance at the Message Origin data. And suddenly my heart is flying out of its chest, my mind dizzy with hope.

"I know who's in that ship."

I take off, diving into the elevator pod, my teammates hot on my heels. I sprint ahead of them, from the Communications Bay to the hatch, and float as fast as humanly possible till I reach the command module. As I push through the hatch door, I remember with a flash how Cyb already fired laser weapons at the "enemy" ship once before. If he does it again—

"Jian!" I point at Cyb, and he manages to restrain the AI just long enough for me to dash to the cockpit's touch screen.

DOCKING REQUEST FROM NEIGHBORING SPACECRAFT, the screen flashes. My whole body trembles as I press Accept.

Every second feels like an eternity as the spacecraft draws closer, the miles between us narrowing . . . until we're close enough for me to see the face in the window.

I'm living a dream as the astronaut looks up, and it's really him. Leo.

The miracle I never dared imagine.

I race to the airlock, ignoring the shouted questions from my dumbfounded crewmates. It feels like my heart is about to fly out of my chest as I wait for him to open the hatch.

It takes longer than it should for him to float through the door, and for one terrible moment, I wonder if this is all a stress-induced hallucination. Am I about to be crushed with disappointment, forced to relive our separation all over again? I mean, how is it even possible that this is real?

But then the hatch swings open. There he is.

All I can feel is my heartbeat, thundering to a crescendo, as we run to each other. We are close enough to touch now, and my skin shivers in anticipation.

Leo reaches his own shaking hand to my cheek, gazing at me as if unsure that I am real. And then my lips are on his, my hands pressing against his back, his fingers running through my hair. He leans his forehead against mine, and as we hold each other close, I feel like I'm flying, free of the ship, free of anything holding me down. That's when I realize we are, in fact, floating in air, our intertwined bodies rising above the floor. And as we gaze at each other, I know one thing for sure: if love can bring Leo halfway across the universe to me, then anything is possible.

I'll never lose hope again.

TWENTY-TWO

LEO

"HALT!"

"Step away from the crew!"

Naomi and I break apart, flushed and confused. And then two heavy steel arms grip my shoulders, yanking me away from her and cuffing my wrists behind my back before I even realize what's happening.

"Cyb." I look up into his empty eyes. "It's Leo Danieli, from Space Training Camp. Don't you remember me?"

But he's not listening. Cyb must have activated his AI Defense Mode, and now he's dragging me across the capsule floor to the airlock.

"You're going back where you came from," he says, his voice cold as ice.

"No! It's safe, it's Leo!" Naomi screams, rushing at Cyb. He tosses her to the side in one effortless motion, and I look around wildly, trying to make eye contact with the rest of the crew gaping at the scene."

"I swear, I'm here for a good reason. Please, you guys— don't let him do this!"

If the others could back us up, if it's not just up to Naomi and me to fend off the raging AI, then I could be free. But they're all just standing there, until—

I gasp as my body slips from Cyb's grip. The handcuffs come off, floating up into the air as my body rises with them, just in time to see Jian pinning the AI to the wall. I stare at him in surprise. I had no clue the dude was that strong—or that he'd care enough to help me. But then I see Naomi beside him, and I realize it wasn't me Jian was trying to help.

I rush forward to join them, and the next few moments are a blur of metal scraping against flesh as we struggle to keep the thrashing robot's arms in place. Naomi's hands shake as she reaches for Cyb's AIOS screen. And then, after pressing a series of buttons on-screen—

"Defense mode cleared."

When Cyb's eyes blink open again, he's like a deflated balloon, all the fight out of him. I drop his arm, while Naomi reaches for mine.

"Come with me," she says. "I'm not letting you get away again."

"Wait." Jian holds up a hand to stop her. "We need

a crew meeting. We have to decide as a team what to do about . . ." He glances at me. "Him."

I realize something is wrong as soon as we're all gathered on the first floor of what Naomi tells me is the Astronauts' Residence. It is dizzying in its bells and whistles, a stark contrast from my utilitarian solo capsule. But something is missing. Someone.

"Where's Dev?"

As the faces around me fall, I feel a pang of fear.

"What? What happened?"

Naomi starts to explain, tears spilling from her cheeks as she recounts what happened on the supply ship. As she speaks, Sydney Pearle's body shudders with sobs, and Naomi wraps a tight arm around her. I stare at the two of them, not wanting to believe it.

"He was my friend," I whisper. "I thought we were all going to be together here."

"What made you so certain you'd be joining up with us, anyway?" Beckett snaps. Clearly he's still the same old jerk as before.

"I wasn't certain. But I hoped."

"I mean, it's a little . . . convenient for Leo to appear right after we lost Dev, isn't it?" Beckett looks around at Sydney, Jian, and Minka. "What reason do we have to trust him?"

"Are you serious?" I sputter. This is a new low, even for Beckett. "Are you actually suggesting—"

"I know you had nothing to do with what happened to

Dev," Sydney says, her eyes devoid of emotion as she looks at me. "But that doesn't mean I want you taking Dev's place, sleeping in his compartment, wearing his uniform . . ." Her voice cracks, and she turns away, covering her face.

"I wouldn't be doing any of that," I tell her gently. "I have my own ship. I would just be joining yours for the trip to Europa so I can help you there . . . if you'll have me."

Jian stares at me like I'm a ghost.

"But how? How are you even here?"

I take a deep breath and begin telling my story. I explain how Greta found me, and I tell them about the map she decoded of Europa's surface ridges and her plan to help the Final Six survive.

"Oh. My. God." Naomi's eyes fill with tears as she stares at me. "It's—it's too incredible to believe. Dr. Wagner's discoveries, and the fact that—that the woman I've looked up to all my life is the one who brought you back to me. . . ." Her voice falters. "I only wish I could have known her, and thanked her for all that she did."

"Me too. She would have loved you."

"Well, it's a nice story and all, but Dr. Takumi and General Sokolov would never sign off on allowing him in," Beckett says, talking about me like I'm not even there. "Leo was cut, remember? And as the person they left in charge, I have to say no. It's our job to put the mission above any one person." He looks me dead in the eye. "You need to go back to Earth, Danieli."

I ignore him, keeping my focus on the other four.

"Dr. Wagner told me from the beginning that my spacecraft had only enough propulsion for a one-way trip, so there's no chance of me going back to Earth. But I was always prepared for the possibility that I might not catch up to you guys, and that I'd remain out here until . . . until my ship couldn't support me anymore. That's my only other option, and I—I'll accept it, if that's what's right for you all. But I believe in everything Greta taught me, and I know I can help the mission."

I glance from one face to the next, trying to gauge which way they're leaning. I won't push myself on them; I can't be that person. But every part of me is desperate for them to say yes.

"There is no scenario where I leave you to flounder in space." Naomi's dark eyes flash with intensity. "I'll die with you here, or we'll travel together to Europa, but I'm never abandoning you. Not after I already left you once."

I don't trust myself to speak. Instead I hold her hand up to my lips, hoping she can feel everything I want to say in my kiss. Jian's face falls.

"Don't do this," he says quietly, looking at Naomi, and I can't tell whether he's talking about us leaving—or her being with me.

"It's crazy," Sydney argues. "You can't just leave—"

"Look what he's doing already," Beckett says, cocking an eyebrow. "He hasn't even been here a full hour and he's already using Naomi as a shield, getting between our crew and dividing us—"

"That's not true." Rage burns under my skin at his words, and I look pleadingly from Minka to Jian and Sydney. "You don't understand what I can bring to the table. You need an underwater specialist who can guide you through Europa's ocean to the Habitable Zone, and I'm the only one who can."

"Let's not forget the whole Habitable Zone theory comes straight from Dr. Wagner, who was taken *off* the mission," Beckett scoffs.

Naomi turns to the rest of the group, ignoring him.

"This isn't a unilateral decision. Let's take a vote. Should Leo and I leave you to continue on to Europa without us, with more resources to share among the four of you? Or should we work as a new team, utilizing Leo's skills and knowledge from Dr. Wagner, and see if we can succeed in the mission together?"

There's an awkward pause, until Sydney raises her hand.

"All else in favor?"

I hold my breath. Jian lifts his hand, followed by Minka. Beckett is the only holdout.

I release the air from my lungs as relief sinks in. Naomi pulls Sydney, Minka, and Jian toward us for a group hug, while Beckett slinks off to the side. I glance at him out of the corner of my eye, curious how he's taking this loss—but he doesn't look as disgruntled as I expected. I wonder if maybe some small part of him didn't want to be responsible for our deaths, after all.

"Um. Guys." Naomi stops still, a smile spreading across

her face. "I just thought of the obvious. Leo . . . I'm guessing your ship has a working X-band antenna?"

"Of course it does," I tell her. "Lark and Asher have been guiding me most of the way."

Naomi slowly turns around, facing the rest of the crew. And to my surprise, they begin cheering at the top of their lungs.

I lead the way through the hatch back to my ship, Naomi's hand in mine the entire time. Even if we weren't already floating in zero g, my feet still wouldn't touch the ground. I'm on the high of my life from achieving the impossible and making it all the way to her, a victory made so much sweeter by the discovery that they actually need me and my ship.

But as soon as we crawl into the capsule, my stomach plummets. Cyb is standing at the helm of my ship—and Kitt is nowhere to be seen. Beside me, Naomi draws in a sharp breath.

"What are you doing here, Cyb?"

The robot pauses and swivels his head to face us. That's when I see the object in his arms: a heavy steel club, aimed straight at my radio receiver.

Naomi drops my hand and takes off running. I race after her, the others hot on our heels as we surround Cyb, blocking him from the radio just as he takes the first swing. The club bashes my shoulder instead, and I yelp as a searing pain burns through my arm. I can barely see straight, but I force my body to remain upright, shielding both Naomi and my comm system from this AI turned violent. And then Jian lunges forward, snatching the club from Cyb's grasp in one impressively quick move. We each grab one of the robot's arms, pinning him against the wall.

"It was you." Naomi stares at the robot with a cold fury. "You destroyed our antenna and cut us off from Earth. Why?"

"You were supposed to be our pilot," Jian spits at Cyb. "How could you, what possessed you, to sabotage the entire mission and our crew like that?"

"It wasn't sabotage," Cyb says calmly. "I was following orders."

"What are you talking about? Whose orders?"

Jian loosens his grip on Cyb and that's when the robot reaches behind his back—and suddenly his ice-blue lenses snap shut. The steady hum of his machinery cuts to silence. And then the platinum and steel exoskeleton tumbles to the floor, pieces breaking apart in a pile of metal. Minka's shriek of horror echoes through the chamber, a look of revulsion on her face as she stares down at the fallen AI.

"What just happened?"

"He decommissioned himself," Naomi says in disbelief. "He's . . . gone."

PART THREE
EUROPA

TWENTY-THREE

I WATCH THROUGH THE WINDOW, HOLDING MY BREATH, AS LEO carries Cyb's remains to the airlock. Even with an EVA suit covering every inch of his skin and a helmet pumping a steady stream of oxygen to his lungs, I still feel a wave of terror as Leo opens the outer hatch. If anything goes wrong—if there's the slightest tear in his suit and he gets exposed to the outside, or if he slips too close to the ledge—then I could lose him as quickly as if he'd never been here at all.

Leo lifts his arms, and the broken pieces of Cyb fly out of his hands and through the open door, reducing Earth's leading artificial intelligence to space junk. It hits me that this marks the third seismic shift in our mission in less than twenty-four hours. From Dev's death to Leo's arrival and

Cyb's self-destruction, we have more changes to adjust to on this one flight than most people deal with in a lifetime.

Leo climbs back through the inner hatch and emerges on my side of the window looking just like the boy I first met at space camp. He's wearing one of his old training uniforms underneath the EVA suit—khakis with a deep blue ISTC crewneck the same color as his eyes. It's like staring straight at the memory I've been holding in my mind all this time. I reach for his hand, needing to reassure myself with his touch that this is still, against all odds, real.

We float side by side to the *WagnerOne* command module, where Jian, Sydney, Minka, and Beckett are crowded around Leo's salvaged radio transceiver. Jian's head snaps up at the sound of our return.

"It's not working—the radio or the internet," he says, agitated.

My stomach seizes, but Leo is calm as he moves up to the cockpit's digital screen.

"It's secured with eye-recognition tech," he explains, floating up close to a red sensor. The sensor turns green and the tablet flashes to life, the radio beside it crackling with promise. My heartbeat speeds up.

"It's ready." Leo glances at me. "Who wants to record the first message for Houston?"

"I'll do it," I answer quickly. "Since I'm communications specialist, I mean. They'll be expecting to hear from me."

Of course that's only a small part of why I volunteered. I need to be the one to explain Leo's presence here. I'm expecting an argument from Beckett as usual, but this time he doesn't object. And then, as I enter the call letters for Houston while mentally planning out what I'm going to say, it hits me why no one else volunteered for this task. As relieved as the world back home will be to learn the five of us are alive—nothing can make up for the fact that Dev isn't. And I'm the one who has to break the news.

"Houston, this is Naomi Ardalan of the *Pontus*. We are back on air and online, thanks to another spacecraft from Earth showing up to help us just in time. It's the late Dr. Greta Wagner's solo ship, commanded by my—by our old friend Leonardo Danieli." I glance at Leo with a smile, imagining the explosive reaction that bit of news will elicit.

"The systems on their ship are invaluable to our mission going forward, and we're grateful to have Leo joining us on the journey to Europa. I will reconfigure our internet to use the *WagnerOne* ship as a communications relay, so that we can once again log on directly from the *Pontus*. So that's . . . that's the good news."

I hesitate. I want to end it right there, to give Earth a reason to celebrate for a change instead of mourning. But I can't. My voice shakes as I recount the hostile living thing aboard the Mars supply ship that killed the *Athena* crew years before killing our own Dev Khanna today.

"Please let his country know that he was—he was so loved," I whisper, fighting back another wave of tears. I clear my throat, forcing myself to stay calm. "Since the *Athena*'s stores of supplies were all contaminated, we're forced to make do with the food that's onboard the *Pontus*. We'll begin using the solar greenhouse to grow nutrients today, and we await further instructions from Houston on how to solve this shortage." I take a deep breath. "And one more thing. If you're looking for Cyb's signal, you won't find it. He's gone, after we discovered he is the one who cut us off from Earth in the first place. He said he was acting on orders—and we would all like to know whose."

I look back at my crewmates, and I can tell we're all thinking the same thing. After what we've seen in the last twenty-four hours, how are we supposed to ever trust anything Dr. Takumi or the general says?

"How long until they receive it?" Minka asks the second I'm done recording.

I glance at the map on-screen. "Based on our current distance from Earth, it'll take about ten minutes for the message to reach them, and then another ten for their reply to get here."

"Good," Leo says, "because I have something to show you in the meantime."

He moves back up to the screen, tapping and swiping until the entire window shield lights up with a digital rendering of Europa. As the moon's red ridges flicker through the screen, Leo traces them with his finger and shows us how to read the ridges as a map.

"Right now, your mission trajectory has the *Pontus* landing at Thera Macula." Leo points to the corresponding location on-screen. "But if we follow Dr. Wagner's primer for reading Europa's surface as a map to extraterrestrial life, we can see that Thera Macula is a dangerously active region. In fact, if you look closely enough, it looks like a . . ."

"A face," I finish his sentence, staring. "It almost looks like the face of some kind of . . . beast."

"Right. But then, if you look over here . . ." His hand moves to another region on the map, one that stands out from the rest, with its unusually bright shade of white and its smooth, flat surface.

"If we follow this band of parallel white ridges to the south, in the area known as Agenor Linea, we don't see any of the red signatures that correspond with alien activity. We also have a saltwater ocean easily accessible to Agenor Linea—which is another reason Dr. Wagner calls this the Habitable Zone."

"The place where we could coexist!" My heart leaps. It's the equation I've been trying to solve all this time—and there's something poetic about my idol being the one to solve it.

"You're not suggesting we completely alter our ship's landing spot based on one woman's wild theory, are you?" Beckett scoffs, back to his usual form.

"She's not one woman," I shoot back. "This is coming from the world's leading scientific mind, someone who actually built a spacecraft for Leo and went to the greatest lengths imaginable to help us. What good reason do we have not to trust her over the same people who led us into that horror show on the supply ship?"

"Well, I can't argue that," Jian acknowledges before glancing up at the countdown clock on the overhead flight mapping screen. He takes a sharp breath. "But if we don't perform this gravity slingshot in the next fifteen minutes, we won't have anywhere to land. Naomi, we need you to check the numbers. Let's go."

"Wait a second!" Minka calls. "What about the reply from Houston?"

"You guys will have to answer it," I tell her, even as the thought of Beckett getting to speak for us makes my stomach queasy. I can only hope Sydney and Minka will do most of the talking.

"C'mon." I grab Leo's hand, and it's like we're floating in fast-forward as the three of us race through the hatches and back to the *Pontus* command module. It's markedly different now, with Tera the only robot on duty, and Jian sliding into Cyb's pilot's seat.

"Naomi, the numbers," he presses.

I hurry to the nearest touch screen, my fingers flying on autopilot as I work through the Kepler equation and the universal variable formulation to determine the new, accurate distance between our geographical coordinates and Europa's, with the *WagnerOne*'s added mass. I work as fast as I can to fill in the correct set of numbers, and five minutes later, Jian is plugging my results into our flight trajectory.

"Okay, you both need to strap into launch seats," he instructs us. "We're about to get hit with an influx of speed."

Our combined ship, the *Pontus* and *WagnerOne* capsules

joined together, starts spinning, closer and closer to Mars—so close that as I stare out the window, it looks as if our entire ship is about to disappear into the red sphere. That's when Jian fires the rockets, kicking the ship's velocity even higher as the *Pontus* turns, entering the path to Jupiter with a massive gravitational push behind us.

And we are on our way.

As the ship hurtles forward on autopilot and the rest of the crew attempts to sleep off the events of the past twenty-four hours, I finally have the alone time with Leo that I've been dreaming of for months—a dream I never thought could actually come true. It's almost like an out-of-body experience as I take his hand, leading him to my room. I make him wait on the bed with his eyes closed while I shower first, the two of us laughing over the sound of running water. I slip into fresh pajama pants and a tank top, and then I lift his hands from his eyes.

"Hi."

"Hi," he whispers. He takes my face in his hands, gazing at me with an expression that floods my cheeks with color, my body with warmth.

"Is this real?" I whisper back, only half joking. As much as I'm aching to fall asleep in his arms, I'm also afraid of what will happen when I wake up. "Will you still be here in the morning?"

He rests his forehead against mine, our lips close enough to touch, and I can feel his curving into a smile.

"I wouldn't be anywhere else in the universe."

As our lips meet, it's like fireworks are exploding in my chest. He wraps his arms around me, and I curl my body into his, savoring the feel of his skin on mine.

And I can't believe I almost went a lifetime without this.

We wake up hours before everyone else, too thrilled by the nearness of each other to sleep, talking without pause as we catch up on the myriad of things we missed in these months apart. After Leo finishes filling me in on life on Earth post–space camp, I lay my head against his chest and ask him about Dr. Wagner. It's still hard for me to fathom that she's gone—that Earth is missing this longtime hero of mine.

"What was she like? I mean, really like, behind the scenes? She always seemed so formal to me, even in her own biography."

"She was that way with me, too," Leo says. "And she could be tough, all business—the kind of person you would never want to cross. But I saw another, private side of her, too. I saw someone as influenced by love and loss as we are." He's quiet for a moment. "No one would describe Greta Wagner as particularly warm, but she was thinking of others in everything that she did. It wasn't about the glory of success with her. She truly wanted to help the Final Six, and I think she saw it as her last purpose."

I smile up at him, moved by his words.

"She picked the right person to help her fulfill it."

"Something else I've been meaning to tell you." Leo shifts onto his side, facing me. "There was one night when I heard what I thought was her playing piano, and it was so surprisingly good that I just had to go upstairs and see if it was really her. So I did, and it turned out to be some automated piano, with the notes playing by themselves—and with every note that played, a different letter or symbol or image flashed on the screen above it. And one of those was . . . my face." Leo shakes his head at the memory. "The way Greta was moving around from the piano to the screen—it was like she was orchestrating the whole thing."

I sit up in bed, staring at him.

"I told you about the signal we received from the Mars supply ship, didn't I?"

"No." He gives me a quizzical look. "What does that have to do with—"

"It came through in musical code," I tell him. "A musical cryptogram—one of the few coded languages I didn't already speak. Minka helped me crack that one."

Leo's eyes widen.

"It did seem like she was writing some kind of coded message. I just didn't know there actually was an existing code."

"Do you remember what any of the symbols were, or looked like?" I reach across him for the old-school notepad and pen I keep on my bedside shelf, and hand them to him.

"I can't remember specific letter or number combinations, but I do remember this."

I peer over his shoulder, and my breath catches when I see what he's sketching.

A double helix.

"She was . . . analyzing your DNA," I say, my heart beginning to race. "The question is . . . why?"

TWENTY-FOUR

LEO

WALKING INTO MY FIRST OFFICIAL DAY WITH THE *PONTUS* crew, I'm a mix of adrenaline and nerves. The larger part of me is itching to dive headfirst into the mission, to learn everything there is to know about life on the *Pontus* and fold myself into the fabric here—become one of them. But a nagging voice reminds me that I wasn't wanted here, that I would be dead if Naomi hadn't used her own leverage to keep me on the ship. My stomach knots up at the thought of facing the other four, and having to prove myself every day to a crew that wishes Dev were standing in my place.

This was never going to be fun and games, I remind myself, as I follow Naomi down to the dining room. I don't need any of these people to be my friend—I just need to focus on the task at hand, my own personal mission for Greta that's wrapped up in theirs.

We arrive to find the dining room empty, and Naomi glances down at her wristband. A message flashes on the screen, and she takes a sharp breath.

"They're in the Communications Bay—with an update from Houston."

My throat turns dry. Looking at Naomi, I can tell she's as nervous as I feel. The ISTC technically still has control over the *Pontus* . . . so how they react to my arrival could impact everything.

She grips my hand, and together we run to the elevator pod. As soon as the elevator doors open onto the first floor, I hear the voice—and my whole body stiffens.

". . . not to be trusted, and your mission cannot afford another mistake."

Dr. Takumi's voice booms through the computer speakers, his words dovetailing with our entrance. Sydney, Jian, Beckett, and Minka all turn to face us, and I flush uncomfortably as their eyes linger on me. I know what they're thinking. I'm the next mistake.

"So what BS is he spinning today?" Naomi says, crossing the room to the computer monitor. Takumi and Sokolov fill the frame, sitting together in one of the NASA offices with matching expressions of concern.

"Good morning, astronauts," Dr. Takumi begins. "It was the relief heard around the world when your message came through. We are thrilled and thankful beyond words to finally hear from you, and know that the five of you are safe. At the same time, our hearts break over the loss of Dev Khanna."

Naomi reaches for Sydney's hand, and my heart twists at the sight of her face—hardening into something different from the Sydney I remembered.

"You can be sure that his life and his sacrifice will be remembered and honored across the Earth, with memorial ceremonies planned in both India and the United States," General Sokolov adds. "If you'd like to write a eulogy of your own, one of us would be glad to read it at the services."

"We want to commend the five of you for continuing to perform your mission duties and keeping your cool in the midst of the unfathomable circumstances thrown your way," Dr. Takumi says. "Your actions and the character you've shown have proven why you were selected for this mission. In the old days of NASA, they used to describe the chosen astronauts as having 'the right stuff.' That certainly applies to you five, and Dev. It's in your DNA."

I shift awkwardly in place. Why do I have a feeling this is about to lead into an unflattering assessment of me?

"Which brings us to Leonardo Danieli." Right on cue. "I don't doubt that his . . . intentions are in the right place. But the scientist who sent him here was a woman in decline, whose mental state severely impaired her judgment and brain functioning—"

My head snaps up.

"That's a lie," I tell the others, my voice shaking with fury. "Greta's mind was as sharp as ever, and her knowledge was so powerful that he and the general wanted her *dead*. And now they're just trying to discredit her—"

Minka shushes me loudly.

"Listen to the rest."

I slump into a seat, folding my arms, as Dr. Takumi continues.

"If he's acting on her commands, then he's not to be trusted, and your mission cannot afford another mistake. I understand how lucky it must have seemed when he showed up, and we certainly appreciate his help enabling the *Pontus* to reestablish ground communication." He pauses. "But it may not be worth the risk of adding an entirely new crewmate whose recent training opposes yours."

"What is he even saying?" Naomi sputters. "Is he actually advocating for—for the murder of Leo?"

"It's not murder when he chose to come here himself," Beckett argues. "He knew the risks."

I can't believe what I'm hearing. I stand and move toward the door, unable to stomach any more. But before leaving, I catch Dr. Takumi's last words.

"As for Cyb . . . All of us at ISTC are deeply disturbed to hear about the AI's malfunction. We're launching a full investigation to determine if a hacker could be responsible for the machine's behavior, and if so, who's the culprit. In the meantime, you did the right thing by disposing of Cyb, though I caution you, Naomi, against keeping the isolated hard drive. If it's been compromised, you don't want a trace of it on the ship."

Naomi's mouth falls open.

"How did he know?"

When the others look at her quizzically, she says in a voice barely above a whisper, "I never said anything in last night's message about keeping the hard drive. The only explanation is that he must have . . . seen me."

"But our ground communications were still dark then, remember?" Minka says. "We didn't connect to Leo's antenna until after Cyb was taken apart."

"Exactly." Naomi looks up, her eyes searching for the blinking overhead camera lights. "What if there was a way to cut us off from Earth—but only one-way? Meaning we couldn't see them and send or receive any messages, but they could see us. What if Takumi and Sokolov have been watching us this entire time?"

"How would they be able to?" I ask from the doorway, too curious about this new wrinkle to leave the room.

"Remember how I was so sure that the AIs came with their own wired-in comm system, independent of our antenna?" Naomi asks the others. "Well, I don't think I was wrong about that. I think . . ." She takes a deep breath. "I think Cyb was following Takumi and Sokolov's command when he destroyed our antenna. It was an inside job. They could have easily controlled him from Houston, including disabling his radio signal when they saw me going to check it. They kept us isolated in this bubble of no contact and fear, and all the while, they were watching."

There's a stunned silence, and I can see from their expressions that Naomi's crewmates don't know what to believe.

Beckett speaks first. "That's an ugly accusation you just leveled at the people controlling our ship."

Naomi lifts her chin.

"Yes. And I'd bet my life that it's true. Why else would Dr. Takumi want me to destroy Cyb's hard drive? I was only keeping it to investigate whose commands he was acting on, and I think it's pretty clear now. If I'm right, better for them to know we've figured out the truth—and we won't be controlled anymore."

"But why would they want to cut us off from communicating with Earth?" Jian shakes his head. "I mean, what would be the point?"

"Information is power, isn't it?" I speak up. "What if there was information they wanted to keep from you . . . maybe even the knowledge that I was on my way?"

Naomi's breath quickens.

"Not only that—my brother was looking into something for me. For us. He was sending me his research on the kinds of alien life that could exist on Europa. The text was encrypted, but what if the messages were still intercepted?"

Beckett groans loudly.

"And what are you suggesting they would have a problem with there? You wasting your time on sci-fi?"

"If Sam was getting warmer, and I convinced you all

of it, we might have bailed on the mission ourselves. That would be the problem." Naomi gives Sydney a meaningful look, as if she knows what Naomi is referring to.

"We're never going to know for sure, though, are we?" Sydney points out. "Not unless they can produce some proof that you're wrong. So all we can do now is . . . keep questioning? Not just blindly follow the authority figures?"

Naomi nods.

"At the very least. We've been through enough, we know enough, to start making our own decisions."

"Is this your full-circle way of saying we should keep Leo on the mission?" Minka says, a snide edge to her voice, and I flinch.

"That's part of it," Naomi admits. "But it's about more than that. From now on, with every step or major decision that needs to be made, I say the answer lies with us—in a group vote. I don't know about you, but I'm done having my fate decided by just one or two more 'powerful' voices."

And as she tosses her hair and strides across the room toward me, head held high—I've never been more in awe.

TWENTY-FIVE

NAOMI

ONE MONTH BEFORE APPROACHING JUPITER ORBIT, THE
energy on the *Pontus* starts to shift. The days that once
seemed to stretch so long are whipping by, full of plans and
preparations: VR simulations to rehearse our upcoming
landing and to practice driving rovers across Europa's rough
terrain and submersibles through her icy waters; mornings
sweating under the lights of the solar greenhouse where we
take turns trying to shore up our food supplies; and, in my
case, reading everything I can get my hands on about the
prehistoric creatures Sam found that resemble the RRB. But
while there's plenty to read about the creatures' physical
attributes, there's nothing to say how they would react to
humans in their midst. On a scale from benign to terrifying,

I don't know whether we're dealing with the likes of dolphins or sharks. But there's one thing I'm sure of: with Leo here, I can face anything.

The *Pontus* has changed for me, too, since his ship docked with ours. Instead of the cold, austere vessel I boarded months ago, the ship now feels like a living, breathing home. There are still two missing pieces: Dev, and the old Sydney. Her grief has formed a shell around her, like a cloak she can't hang up. And I know why she avoids Leo and, by extension, me. She can't stand to be around the person who unwittingly took his place. I wish there was something, anything, I could do to make it better—but as my mom would say, time fixes all. I just have to wait.

The morning of "T-minus thirty days" is the same milestone date when we're expected to double up our RRB doses, to guard against the punishing radiation ahead. Instead of sharing a table with Leo, I slide in next to Sydney at breakfast. She peers up at me over her book with a "Can I help you?" expression, and I feel a twinge in my chest, remembering when we used to be friends.

"What should we do?" I ask under my breath. "With what we know about the RRB, doesn't it seem like a dangerous move to increase the doses? I mean, it already feels like we're taking a giant risk every time we inject just a low dose of the serum . . ."

"I don't know." Sydney fiddles with her curls, thinking. "I've spent a lot of time weighing the pros and cons, but the one inescapable fact is that Europa's radiation will torch us if we don't have the antidote. And, creepy as this one is . . . well, it hasn't hurt any of us here so far, has it?"

"But how do we know the dosage amount isn't all that's keeping us from ending up like Suki or Callum?" I worry.

"We don't. But until you can think of another way to solve the radiation problem, I'm going to have to follow the rules on this one. And, who knows." She gives me a wry half smile. "Maybe having some of those alien cells in our blood will turn out to be a good thing."

"Hard to imagine that," I say with a shudder.

I can barely watch as Sydney sinks the needle into Jian's arm that night. Leo reaches for my hand, and though we usually make a point of avoiding PDA around the others, this time I hold tight to his palm. I'm dreading the moment when it's us up there, but more than that, I'm afraid of the unknown after.

I squeeze my eyes shut when it's my turn, not wanting to look as the alien blue serum pierces through my skin. But I soon realize it was a mistake to close my eyes.

I'm swimming straight into a climbing, breathing black fog. Puffs from the rising cloud fill my lungs, foreign parti-cles crawl against my skin, and I wonder if anyone will hear if I scream underwater—

"Naomi! You okay?" Sydney's hand grips my arm. "You're sweating."

I blink, and the scene vanishes.

"Y-yeah," I mumble. "That was just . . . weird."

It was like the vision I had right after my first shot in space. Only this time, it seems to pick up right where the other left off.

T-Minus Twenty-Four Hours Till Europa

Our last night on the ship brings the six of us together in a way we haven't been before. It's Jian who suggests we make a final visit to the Observatory as a group, and we stop there before dinner, pressing our hands against the glass and comparing the goose bumps forming across our skin at the sight. After everything we've been through, it's surreal to be this close to our final destination—close enough now to see Jupiter's massive swirl of color as the dazzling gas giant rotates in the distance. And I know I'm a different Naomi today than I was in those first weeks when I'd linger here, desperate for home.

While the Observatory visit is full of giddy excitement, dinner is when the nerves start to creep back as reality closes in: we are about to leave the cocoon of the ship and set foot on an alien world—where anything can happen.

None of us six manages to eat more than a bite of our last dinner on the *Pontus*, and when the lights power off for bed, I can only toss and turn. Finally, after hours of struggling to fall asleep, I slip out of my cabin and make my way through the ship to the airlock, climbing out the other side to the sight that always makes me smile.

I find Leo restlessly pacing his flight capsule, checking different dials on the control panel even though there's no need—the *Pontus* is steering him now. But when he sees me, his face relaxes, and the worry lines disappear.

He takes my hand, leading me back to the one-man crew quarters, with its single bunk bed, small kitchen table, gym equipment, and tiny makeshift lounge area.

"I still can't believe you stuck it out in here all those weeks before making it to Mars, not even knowing if Greta's plan would work." I shiver. "We could have missed each other in space. We—"

"But we didn't." He laces his fingers in mine. "It worked out . . . just like it will on Europa."

"I hope so." I swallow hard. "Did you know that landing a spacecraft is statistically the most dangerous part of a mission?"

He pauses.

"Where are you going with this?"

"Well, how . . . how do we know we'll survive tomorrow?"

"We don't know," Leo concedes. "But I believe we will. If anyone has a fighting chance of surviving, well—I think we've proven it's us." He wraps his arm around me, pulling me in close. "And if this is our last night . . . then I'm just glad to be spending it with you."

I look up at him with a smile.

"I love you, you know."

Leo gives me a grin that nearly melts my insides.

"I love you, too."

"Do you ever wish that we could just . . . be together,

without the colossal stress of trying to survive in space? You know, like normal couples before the world went mad: going on dates, sharing ordinary things like our favorite foods, TV shows, music . . ." I trail off.

"All the time," he answers. And then he stands up straighter, a sudden light glimmering in his eyes. "How about . . . now?"

"Now?" I raise an eyebrow at him, gesturing at the space around us. "This doesn't exactly scream 'normal date night atmosphere.' Especially considering the fact that we're somewhere with literally no atmosphere."

"I know imagination doesn't come naturally to scientists," he teases me. "But just for tonight, pretend you're with me in Rome." He moves closer, running his hand up and down my cheek, and I lean into him, closing my eyes. "You're at my apartment on Via Piacenza, I've poured you an aperol spritz . . ."

I giggle as he reaches over to a cabinet and pulls out two gravity-mimicking Space Cups and packets of lemonade. He pours us each a glass, and raises his toward mine. "*Saluti.*"

I clink my glass against his, and then he turns to the desktop computer.

"Now for mood music . . ."

I stop still, my mouth falling open, as a song I could never forget starts to play over the speakers.

"Te voglio bene assai,
ma tanto tanto bene sai."

Leo pulls me in for a slow dance, his hands encircling my waist. I wrap my arms around his neck. "Almost normal," I whisper with a smile.

He hums along, just as I imagined he would back when he sent me the song. His warm breath tickles my ear, and I lift my chin, tilting my face to his.

"A bond that melts the blood inside the veins," I whisper.

His smile widens at the realization that I know what the lyrics mean. And then we are giving in to the words, the melody, the moment, as our lips meet over and over again.

T-Minus Sixty Minutes Till Landing

The moment we've been waiting for, fearing and anticipating all these months—is finally here.

The six of us take our positions in the flight deck: Jian seated at the cockpit beside Tera, who's remained stationed here ever since Cyb was deprogrammed, and the rest of us strapped into our acceleration seats. After Jian makes the argument that it'll help our velocity to ditch the *Wagner-One* in orbit and have Leo and Kitt join us in the capsule for landing, Leo slips into the empty seat next to me. And I can tell as he looks at me that we're both thinking the same thing: the person the seat belonged to first. But our mission affords no time to linger on the past. The future is hurtling toward us, in the form of an icy, red-splintered moon.

The ship's interior starts rattling violently as we spiral closer to Jupiter—so close that it looks like we could reach out and touch the gas giant. While Tera and Jian narrate the action through their headsets, the rest of us watch from the ceiling video screen, and I let out a gasp at the sight of our solar panel wing skimming past Jupiter. The biggest planet in the solar system is now in our rearview.

And then the ghostly white face of Europa takes center stage.

"Beginning orbital transfer," Tera announces. We're soaring down now, over a rocky, red-streaked landscape. "Pitching descent."

The *Pontus* shudders and pitches downward as the capsule fills with screams. I grip Leo's hand, feeling like my stomach is flying out of my body. I force myself to focus on the screen above, on the sights—and I can't help noticing that the closer we get to the ground, the more the rocky white landscape and crevasses resemble skeleton bones.

"Landing gear ready," Tera continues. "We now have eyes on our target landing site. Approaching Thera Macula—"

"What?"

The robot's words send a shock wave through the cabin. Tera must have rerouted our destination . . . to the exact location we were trying to avoid.

I hear Jian panicking, jabbing at different buttons to try to change the landing site back to Agenor Linea—but he can't even log in to the Flight Navigation program anymore.

"I'm locked out!" he yells. "The computer is saying that only Houston Mission Control has access. We're stuck, and we—"

"Initiating capsule separation," Tera drones. "Deploying

landing gear. Final stage separation and descent in five . . . four . . ."

A green light illuminates the control panel. It's too late. We're landing on Thera Macula—alien territory. And there's nothing we can do about it.

"Final stage separation and descent in three . . . two . . ."

The spacecraft splits in two, its engines and power propulsion modules falling away, into the vacuum—

". . . One!"

The remainder of the *Pontus* drops its last thousand feet, the thrusters unfurling, claws of machinery driving toward the ice below. And then the ship comes slamming to a stop.

For the first time in a year, everything is still.

TWENTY-SIX

LEO

MINKA IS THE FIRST TO BREAK THE SILENCE WITH A CRY OF disbelief that pierces the cabin. I pull off my helmet with shaking hands and turn to the rest of the crew. It hits me now that each of us, at one point or another, doubted we'd ever make it to Europa alive. And now, against the odds . . . here we are.

I can't tell who makes the first move, but as soon as we hear the click of a safety restraint unbuckling, the rest of us follow suit. There's the rustling of heavy fabric as our six bodies rise up off the launch seats, and we stumble together through the new microgravity, toward the window shield at the front of the cabin. That's where we catch our first glimpse of the icy, red-streaked ground.

I squeeze my eyes shut and open them again, unsure if I'm awake or dreaming. For the first time, Europa isn't just a picture or a model—it's the land our ship is standing on.

Beckett lets out an expletive-laden cheer, his fists in the air like an Olympian who just won gold.

"We. Did. It! No other achievement in human history can touch what we just accomplished! First effing humans to land on Europa!!"

And suddenly, as Jian and Sydney whoop and cheer along with him and Naomi flies into my arms, the energy in our cabin shifts from fear to euphoria. It's like we've forgotten that we should be terrified, forgotten all our differences and tensions, as the six of us hug and cry and jump up and down—together.

Only the two robots manage to keep calm. It makes me laugh out loud to see Tera and Kitt, dutifully running through their Disembarking Checklist while Jian pops the bottle of bubbly stored for just this occasion, the rest of us cheering at the top of our lungs. And then, after we've filmed the icy view outside our window and recorded our first historic message to beam back to Earth, all while gulping down champagne—there's only one thing left to do.

Go outside.

As soon as Jian mentions opening the airlock, the celebration freezes.

"Can't we just . . . enjoy this one victory a little longer before going out there?" Sydney asks with a shiver. "I mean, I still don't know what I believe, but—what if Dr. Wagner was right? What if we really did just land in the most dangerous spot?"

There's a long pause. I can tell that the prospect of venturing beyond our safe haven puts all of us, even Beckett, on edge. But we can't hide out in the spaceship forever.

"It's not like we can launch back into orbit and fix our destination," Jian points out. "We don't have the fuel or propulsion left. If we decide to make the trip to Agenor Linea, we'll have to drive there by rover. Which means, either way, we're going outside."

"One of us should go first, to get the lay of the land and see what we're walking into, before everyone else leaves the ship," I say. "And it should be me. The rest of you were actually chosen for this mission, so your safety comes first." I crack a smile. "I'm here to be the guinea pig."

"I'll go with you," Naomi offers, but I shake my head.

"No. I have to do this alone."

Beckett raises an eyebrow at me, and I wonder if he'll refuse, not wanting anyone else to claim the honor of being the first to walk on Europa. But he stays silent, which only adds to my nerves. He's not fighting my decision—because he knows I'm taking the biggest risk.

Naomi and Kitt help me into the multilayer pressurized Europa space suit, attaching the hard fiberglass shell to my torso that sustains my upper body and life-support backpack, and securing the Extravehicular Visor over my helmet. I switch on the lights and cameras inside the visor, check the suit pressure for any leaks, and then—it's time.

I walk forward, alone.

The airlock unseals with a hiss, and my heart rises in my throat at the first sliver of light through the opening door. A close-up of something silver turns into a tapestry of ice as the scene widens, until I can see it all—the new world, spread out before me.

There is so much to look at, I can't focus my eyes in one place—not on the sky, dominated by the jaw-dropping enormity of Jupiter; or the ground, where red-veined ice awaits its first touch. My surroundings take on the surreal, blurred quality of dreams and I blink rapidly, trying to clear my vision, as a voice in my head nudges me to move. But I'm frozen in place, my legs as rigid as the landscape in front of me.

The lander's side door shudders open, and a short flight of stairs unfurls. The sound jolts me out of my trance, and I step forward, making my way down the stairs in what feels like slow motion.

This is it. The thousands of astronauts who trained and dreamed before me, the billions of dollars devoted to the space program over the last century, were all leading up to this—a moment I'm fairly certain I'm not worthy of. The best I can do is come close.

I'm at the final stair now. I take a deep breath behind my helmet, readying for the first step. And then my boots meet the ice.

I gasp at the feel of solid ground beneath me, a practically foreign feeling after months of moving floors and floating corridors. But no sooner have my feet touched the ground than I'm back in the air again, my body bounding forward from the microgravity like some kind of wily cartoon character. I laugh out loud, the sound reverberating across the empty landscape. And then my laughter turns to tears as it hits me just how far I've come from where my family left me—so far, I'm not sure their spirits could find me here. But I know they would be proud of who I've become, how much I've changed since those desperate months alone in Italy.

"There it is," I murmur into my headset. "The first human steps on Europa."

I try to think of something else to add for posterity, something as poetic as Neil Armstrong's "one small step" line from a century ago. But all I can do is whisper in my home language, "*Bellissimo.*"

And it's true. Europa might be all jagged ice and rock, but there is still something starkly beautiful about it. Especially when you look at the sky: half of it ablaze with color from Jupiter, while the other half remains shrouded in darkness. It's like day and night existing at once, splitting the same sky. Even the most extensive training and mock-ups couldn't have prepared me for that.

A sudden chill runs through my body, and that's when it hits me: the miraculous reality that I'm actually outside again. There are no tight confines out here, no walls bearing down on me. Even the shock of the cold, biting enough to feel through my heated space suit, is a welcome change. After months of living in a perfectly regulated, temperature-controlled flying machine, I'd almost forgotten what extreme temperatures felt like. Now the chill makes me feel more human—more alive.

"Tell us everything." Naomi's voice bursts through my headset. "What does it look like from your point of view, what does it feel like?"

"I could get used to this feeling, actually," I say with a grin as my body springs effortlessly across the red ridges. "Turns out microgravity is a lot more fun than zero g."

I come to a halt as my path splits in two, with one long artery in the ice jutting to the right. After a moment's hesitation, I make the turn. And then, after a ten-minute stretch of the same blank canvas, the scene changes. I stop in my tracks at the forest of ice spikes looming before me.

"Whoa," I whisper into the headset. "Are you guys seeing this through my cam?"

"The penitentes," Sydney's voice breathes. "They're so much bigger than I thought. . . ."

I hear Naomi urging me to be careful, but I'm already moving, the microgravity landing me at the entrance to the ice forest in just two leaps. Towering silver-white blades rise up on all sides of me, rows and rows of them, engulfing me like an ant in a field.

"We just lost you in our direct sight line," Jian says sharply. "Come out of the spikes, Leo."

"Wait. I've never seen anything like this. . . ." My voice trails off as I crane my neck to look up at the soaring ice. "They're all uniform—the same height, the jagged edges in the same places. What are the odds of that?"

"We'll check it out later when you have backup," Naomi says hurriedly. "Come back to the ship, Leo, please."

The worry in her voice gets me, and I turn back—but not before reaching my gloved hand to one of the spikes. And then I draw back my hand in shock.

Something just . . . stung me.

I frantically study my glove, breathing a sigh of relief when I see that it wasn't punctured. That was lucky. But then . . . if nothing penetrated my glove, how to explain what I just felt?

"My hand," I mutter into the headset as I weave past the spikes. "I felt this—this hot stinging through my palm when I touched the spike. I still feel it . . . but my glove wasn't breached."

"You touched the spike?" I hear Naomi exclaim, while Minka says calmly, "It's just your imagination. You couldn't feel something like that through your gloves. If anything, maybe you were just anticipating the extreme cold of the ice, like the sting of frostbite."

"Yeah," I say doubtfully. "Maybe."

"So is there anything else?" Beckett's derisive voice cuts in. "Anything more interesting to show us than ice spikes? Where are the aliens you were so insistent on helping us with? I thought you and Greta Wagner said this was supposed to be the 'Extraterrestrial Hot Zone' or something." He snorts.

I stop still, clenching my fists.

"You really think discovering life happens that fast? We haven't even been here a full hour."

"Long enough to know it's a wasteland," Beckett says. "Look around you. The only thing alive on Europa is us."

I open my mouth to argue, but then I realize . . . I have no comeback. It kills me to admit Beckett could be right about anything, but I don't see or hear a single sign of activity. The entire landscape is devoid of life. Then again, we've only just scratched the surface. The others might be quick to write off Dr. Wagner—but I still believe.

Back at the lander, the others step out of the airlock one by one to join me. First is Jian, who takes one look at Jupiter above us and the rocky ice below, and lets out a victory yell—the most unrestrained I've seen Jian since the day he learned he'd lost his family. Sydney follows him, and when the microgravity knocks her off her feet, she doesn't try to get up. She stays kneeling on the ice as if in prayer, running her gloved hands across the alien ground. And then Naomi comes stumbling toward me, her expression frozen in awe behind her glass faceplate. For everything the six of us have experienced up to this point, nothing comes close to *this*— stepping into the new world that was once far more fantasy than fact.

"Look."

Naomi grips my gloved palm in hers, and I follow her gaze to the lander steps. My mouth falls open at the sight of Tera and Kitt, their mechanical bodies morphing the second they step onto the ice. Their limbs lengthen, thick blades form beneath their feet, and a clear plastic coating falls across the metal masks that make up their faces, unraveling and shaping itself to their bodies. And then the two AIs glide smoothly across fractured ice with none of our human clumsiness, instantly adapted to our new environment.

"Greta thought of everything," I say, swallowing the lump in my throat.

Beckett and Minka are the last to emerge, and when Beckett touches the ground, it's without his usual cocky swagger. The magnitude of this place has humbled us all.

The six of us and our two AIs stand side by side, facing the pale landscape ahead. And then Minka asks what we're all thinking.

"So . . . what happens now?"

Jian glances back at the lander, its hefty cargo bay holding the supplies to keep us alive.

"Now we build."

The empty ice transforms into a hub of activity, with the crew and two AIs hauling cargo out of the lander while Tera directs us to where the X is marked: the spot on the Europa map chosen long ago for our surface habitat. Except . . . the path they're following is the one I was sent here to interrupt.

Everyone else is in motion: Sydney and Minka assembling the first solar panel to get us powered up and online, while Beckett and Jian haul out heaps of aluminum and canvas that will inflate to become an eighteen-hundred-square-foot temporary home. Meanwhile, Naomi and I huddle off to the side, debating what to do.

"I could just run into the lander, unload the rovers, and insist we follow Greta Wagner's map instead, before we get in too deep here—" I start to say when Jian's voice crackles through my headset.

"Leo! Beckett!" He beckons us toward him. "You two were the ones trained in using the nuclear hydrothermal drill—now's your chance to use it. Naomi, Minka needs your help linking her computer with the drill system for the first sample analysis."

My stomach drops. Naomi and I exchange a look of alarm.

"You—you want to drill through the ice here? What about everything Greta Wagner warned me—us—about this location? Who knows what life is under there, what it'll do—"

"Give it a rest, Danieli." I can practically hear the eye roll through Beckett's voice. "We caused the biggest disturbance already when we landed. If there was any life to worry about, it would have shown itself by now."

From across the ice, I see Jian glance at Naomi with an apologetic shrug.

"You know I was willing to change course for Wagner's theory, but now that we're here—well, it seems Dr. Takumi and General Sokolov were right. It's just what they said it would be: empty, untouched. And since it'll take days to melt the ice, we need to start now."

"But what about *underneath* the ice?" I press. "For all we know, we could be waking a sleeping giant under there."

Jian hesitates, and I cross my fingers that I'm getting through to them.

"We should all have a say, remember?" Naomi speaks up, her voice firm. "So. All in favor of taking the rovers to the safer zone indicated by Greta Wagner and drilling there instead?"

Ours are the only two hands that go up. I turn to give Naomi a half-hearted smile. At least we tried. There's nothing I can do now but pull my weight—especially if my role here turns out to be as pointless as Beckett would like to believe.

I force myself to look my rival in the eye.

"Let's do this, then."

"You don't know how to get into the vault where the drill probe is stored," he says with a smirk. "I'll go into the lander to launch it. You can stay on the ice to set up the first sample collection."

"Fine."

I wait, my palms sweating in their gloves despite the cold. And then, more than ten minutes later, the ground starts rumbling. A long mechanical arm swings forward from the side of the lander, like a sharp-toothed cousin of the *Pontus*'s Canadarm. I jump into action, grabbing a test tube from my supply pack and attaching it to the drill blades, before guiding it onto the ice.

"Go!" I shout into my earpiece. And then the rotating blades start to gnash their teeth against the ice, while jets within the drill shoot out heated water to speed up the thawing. I can't look away from the sight.

I feel a warmth beside me and glance up to see Naomi. As her gloved hand slips into mine, I know we are thinking the same thing.

If there really is life on Europa—the life Greta Wagner wrote and theorized about; that Naomi spent her entire time at space camp investigating—we'll find it right here.

Later, while the robots finish unpacking the lander, the six of us assemble our habitat under the light of Jupiter, firing air into industrial-strength canvas using pressure equalization valves. Watching the canvas transform into the walls and ceilings of a home is another surreal moment in a sea of them as we put into action what we practiced during space camp training a lifetime ago. And then Minka's computer emits a series of beeps.

She and Naomi drop the half-inflated corners they're holding and dash over to the folding table that we're using as a makeshift data-analysis station. The rest of us crowd around them, holding our breath as Minka swipes the screen.

"The first sample results are in!"

She peers forward, and her whole body turns rigid—just as Naomi gasps and grabs Minka's arm. It seems they've both arrived at the same discovery. My heartbeat speeds up as I watch them.

"Well? What is it?" Beckett nudges his way forward, staring at the screen.

"The water." Minka's voice wavers. "It's—not normal."

"What do you mean?" Jian's voice rises in panic. "Are you saying it's not safe to drink?"

"No. I might be saying the opposite." Minka studies the letters and numbers on-screen, her eyes wide. "Look what was found in our first drill sample here."

She points to a row of symbols, her hand resting on a chemical formula I don't recognize offhand: $C_{12}H_{22}O_{11}$.

"Sucrose," Naomi whispers. "A food source."

My jaw drops.

"Seriously?" Sydney stares from Naomi to Minka in disbelief. "You're saying the ocean contains naturally derived sugar?"

"We have to do more testing to confirm, but it looks good." Minka smiles at us, a giddy look in her eyes that I haven't seen before.

"Too good," I say slowly, fixing my gaze on Naomi. "What are the odds of us stumbling upon that kind of miracle?"

"Except we didn't really stumble on it," Beckett says. "Why do you think Dr. Takumi and the general were so insistent on this location?"

His words stun us into silence. But if they knew . . . why keep it a secret?

"That's why they were willing to put the Final Six through every risk," Naomi says numbly. "A new world with its own natural food resource and water ocean, wrapped in one? That's too rich a prospect to miss—even if it means sacrificing us in the process."

"It was only a theory until now," Beckett says, gazing at the computer screen in awe. "Nothing definite enough to announce, in case they ended up being wrong and disappointing the world. But they had some data that hinted at this—enough to discuss it at the White House." A smile spreads across his face. "And now I—we—get to tell them all that we discovered it."

"Well, hold the celebration," Naomi says flatly. "Because wherever there's nutrients, there's life, to feed on it. And whatever that life is, we can't expect it to willingly share its food and water and world with us."

For once, Beckett doesn't have a comeback at the ready. And then Minka turns on her heel, away from our half-constructed home.

"I'm going to go get the imaging spectrometer from the cargo bay. It'll help us see the composition of the ocean in even more detail. . . . Be right back."

"All right." Jian picks up one of the pressure equalization valves. "Back to work."

Hardly anyone speaks while we finish inflating the Hab, though there's an electric energy running through us. I know our minds are all occupied with the same thing: the water, and what it means. But in my case, there's something else I can't stop thinking about. Did Greta have any clue about this? If so, why keep it from me? And if not . . . then is there something else important she might have missed? Was she right, or was she wrong about Thera Macula, and the reason I'm here?

It feels like hours later when the loud popping sounds from our inflating Hab suddenly cease, and Naomi lets out a little whoop.

"You guys, it's done!"

A sprawling rectangular structure stands upright on the ice, the size and shape of a family home back on Earth, but with round airlocks instead of doors. I stare ahead in wonder. Looking at it now, it's hard to believe this sturdy, spacious place was nothing but a heap of canvas just hours ago.

"Impressive," Jian says with a grin. "Let's go claim our bunks!"

We rush forward, spirits high at the prospect of getting to go inside and ditch our helmets and bulky space suits in this new, oxygen-pumping habitat. But before we make it to the first airlock, Naomi says, "Shouldn't Minka be back by now?"

The question stops us all in our tracks.

"How long has it been?" I ask. "She was just going to get a science instrument from the cargo bay, right?"

"Half an hour, maybe more?" Beckett guesses. "Let's just radio her to come back already."

Naomi glances down at her wrist monitor and taps the mini-screen until Minka's name and photograph pop up.

"Minka, it's Naomi. We're waiting for you at the habitat. Do you copy?" She waits a beat, and then repeats the message. Nothing. My stomach tightens.

"Tera, do you copy? Have you or Kitt seen Minka by the lander?"

"No," Tera's voice echoes through our headsets. The five of us exchange uneasy looks. And then Naomi claps a hand over her mouth.

"L-look what just happened."

She holds up her wrist monitor for all to see. There on the Contacts screen, in bold red letters flashing across Minka's face, are the words: DEVICE DISCONNECTED.

"What?" My heart starts hammering in my chest. What could have happened to her?

"We have to go find her," Jian says, his face turning ghastly pale.

"We should split up to cover more ground," I tell him. "Maybe you and Sydney and Beckett can search the area around the lander, and Naomi and I will take the other side of the surface."

Jian nods, and Naomi and I break into a run, our pace

marred by stumbles from the microgravity. It's a few minutes before I realize where we're running to—the forest of ice spikes. And then Naomi lets out a strangled scream, stopping dead in her tracks.

"What? What is it?"

She points downward with a shaking hand. And that's when I see it: a glowing, crimson light moving underneath the red ridges—like a snake slithering through a tunnel.

"Oh, God."

"Bioluminescence," Naomi whispers into her headset, eyes widening with terror. "It's life—we've just found life on Europa."

I choke back a scream of my own as the glowing red light skitters beneath our feet.

"Get back," I cry, pulling her behind me. "Go back to the Hab, where it's safe. I'll be there soon."

"No way—"

I dart forward between the spikes, Naomi shouting my name behind me. But there's no sign of Minka here; only the field of towering ice blades. And this time, as my shoulder brushes against the side of one of the blades, I feel another sharp, searing sting.

"Minka." I open my mouth to call her name, but I feel suddenly drowsy . . . like I don't have the energy left to speak. My legs are sinking, I'm falling back against the ice—

And then another body rushes in, one arm circling my waist, the other shouldering my weight.

"Don't touch anything," Naomi says frantically as she

helps me through the maze of penitentes. "Whatever you do, don't touch the ice spikes."

We just barely make it back to the Hab, before I collapse onto the floor. Three fearful faces stare back at us.

Minka's gone.

TWENTY-SEVEN

"IT'S ALIVE."

I turn to my remaining crewmates, huddled on the floor of the half-empty Hab. They watch warily as Sydney examines Leo's shoulder and he winces in pain, while Tera and Kitt stand guard, one AI posted at each airlock. The tense, terrified atmosphere couldn't be further from the celebratory mood of just a few hours ago, and it's hard to believe this is the same place—that we're the same us.

"That's the phrase Suki kept repeating, in Mandarin, the night of her RRB reaction," I continue. "And now I know

271

what she meant. It wasn't just the bacteria that was alive. It's Europa."

"What are you talking about?" Sydney asks numbly.

"The ice spikes, the red ridges—there's life in all of it. Some of it might be microscopic, like whatever is living on the spikes that stung Leo, but it's alive all the same. And what I saw, the flash of color moving under the ice . . ." My voice catches at the memory, and I squeeze my eyes shut, trying to will the image out of my mind.

"As long as that . . . thing is alive," Leo says quietly, "then we might not be much longer."

Beckett stands up suddenly.

"The ice—we still have the drill running. We have to disable it."

Too little too late, buddy, I feel like retorting. But if there was ever a time for me to swallow my grudges, it's now.

"None of us are leaving the Hab until we better assess our risk," Jian says firmly.

"Since when did you become the authority here?" Beckett snaps. "Did you forget who Takumi and Sokolov left in charge?"

"If you think any of that matters now, you're deluded," Jian shoots back, and I resist the urge to applaud. But Beckett stares him down without flinching.

"It matters plenty. Considering I'm the only one who has any clue how to obliterate the monsters."

Now he has everyone's full attention.

"What are you saying?" I ask, my heart beginning to race. "Does this have to do with your so-called 3D-printing lab?"

"I drew the sword," he says, looking away. "Now I have to wield it."

For a second I think he's just trying to be annoying, talking in riddles. But then I remember the book gifted to him by his powerful family at our livestreaming videoconference: *He Who Drew the Sword*. What if that book, that title, actually meant something—something he's trying to tell us now?

"Is this a literal or figurative sword we're talking about here?" I press.

"What I'm saying is that I was chosen." Beckett meets my eyes. "To lead the group—and to kill whatever threat we might find here. So unless you want our mission to end in complete failure, you'll listen and follow my lead."

There's a long pause, and I know the four of us are wondering the same thing. Is he for real?

"And what are you planning to kill these aliens with?" Sydney challenges him. "I haven't seen a single weapon come out of the cargo bay since we landed, so I'm thinking you must be full of it."

Even at a moment this dire, Beckett can't resist a smirk.

"That's because you didn't know where to look. None of you did."

His tone raises the hair on the back of my neck.

"You've seen the mini-submersibles a dozen times in the cargo bay, haven't you? And yet you passed right by them, without even realizing what they are." Beckett leans forward, and I can tell from his expression that he's been waiting a long time to reveal this secret.

"What if I told you that, hidden within the subs, are underwater drones—armed with a toxic blend of Earth chemicals—that could wipe out an entire ecosystem?"

My mouth falls open. I hear Jian swear under his breath.

"You'd better be kidding," Sydney says shakily. "What kind of masochist would bring toxic waste onto a space mission that's already the riskiest of its kind? Did we really need to add more life-and-death stakes here?"

"Don't be so dramatic." Beckett rolls his eyes at her. "The drones can't even detonate until they're fully sub-merged in water. So unless you plan on hanging out with the ETs below the ice, you're safe." He lifts his chin proudly. "The first prototype came in from General Sokolov and Roscosmos right before our launch, and then I used the 3D lab to print replicas—so now we have an arsenal."

"This is—it's madness," I sputter. "If what you're saying is true, then you're talking about chemical warfare and exterminating an entire population! You do realize that's the definition of evil, right?"

"Is it? Because I'm following orders from people who know a hell of a lot more than you," Beckett says evenly. "And after what happened to Minka—"

"We don't know what happened to her," Sydney

interrupts. "She could still be out there."

"And we're wasting time," Jian says, gritting his teeth in frustration. "Beckett, forget about your drones, at least for now. I'm asking Tera to take over and disable the drill, and also continue the search for Minka. She's trained in what to do, and if the worst should happen, I think we would all rather not lose another crew member."

I exchange a worried glance with Leo, the two of us knowing exactly what this means. If anything does happen, this will be the last time we see Tera. And with Kitt set to deactivate any day now when his memory and battery run their course—that would leave us without any artificial intelligence. Something no space mission has had to contend with since the twentieth century.

Minutes later, as Tera unseals the airlock and disappears outside, Beckett stands up and starts to pace, turning his disgruntled gaze on me.

"Shouldn't you at least finish setting up our internet and radio comm system? It's crazy that no one back home has a clue what's going on here."

"We're lucky to have any power at all," I answer sharply. "We were still only halfway through the solar panel setup when Minka went missing. Until it's safe to go outside, we can't risk it."

"So you'd have us just trapped in this glorified tent indefinitely?" Beckett exclaims.

"That's it." Jian steps between us. "We're all on edge, and aside from the obvious reasons, we also haven't slept in, what, thirty hours? I know it seems impossible, but we should try to get some rest. We need to be alert for—for whatever comes next."

"But what about Minka and Tera?" Sydney asks. "Shouldn't we wait for them?"

I catch Jian's eye, and I know he's thinking the same thing as me.

"If either of them is coming back," he says, "they'll know how to access the outer airlock."

Beckett stalks away, grumbling about how he'll be busy formulating a plan while the rest of us "softies" sleep, and I reach out my hand to help a still-weakened Leo to his feet. I can't imagine getting a wink of sleep with the horrors just outside our door, but I know Jian is right. We have to at least try—especially Leo.

We make our way to the row of inflated temporary bunks, one word echoing in my head with every step.

If. If Tera is alive. If Minka is, somehow, alive.

And if we will be, after tonight.

The airlock bursts open. I jolt awake at the clanging sound, panic turning to relief as I realize what this means. Tera succeeded, we have our AI back—

"Minka!"

My hand flies to my mouth at the sound of Sydney's cry. That's a whole other miracle I hadn't predicted.

I leap out of bed, nearly colliding with Leo on the way.

We seize hands and race to the airlock, not stopping for breath until we see the pale blond figure in front of the hatch, surrounded by Sydney and Jian. And then I'm running again, throwing my arms around Minka.

"You're alive!" I babble, giddy with relief. "You're really ali—"

I stop midsentence, a shudder running through me. Her body is so cold against mine. Cold enough to sting.

"Thank God you're okay," Leo breathes, staring at her. "What—what happened?"

But Minka doesn't answer. She just stares straight ahead. I exchange a worried look with the others.

"Did you hurt your head or something?" I ask.

She blinks at the sound of my voice, but still no reply. I look closer at Minka. There's something different about her, something . . . robotic. Her blue eyes are vacant. And I am more afraid than ever.

"You're back!"

Beckett comes running behind me, the most genuine smile I've ever seen on his face. Before I can warn him, he's pulling her in for a bear hug, and I watch as her face registers no emotion in response.

"What's—what happened?" he asks, looking down at her uncertainly.

Minka makes a move toward the airlock door . . . and gestures for us to follow.

"Um. That's not a good idea," Jian speaks up. "You only

just came back, and we still have Tera out there, trying to assess the risk outside—"

But Minka keeps moving, and Beckett rushes behind her.

"She's trying to tell us something, or show us something. Let's go."

"No, we—"

But it's too late. Beckett is already pulling his EVA suit down from the wall and throwing on his helmet. I hear Leo swear in Italian before doing the same.

"No," I whisper before turning to Sydney and Jian. "You two, stay here. Whatever you do, just keep yourselves safe."

I hear them calling for me to stay, but I can't; I can't let them go out there alone, without a scientist. I force one foot in front of the other, fear churning like a virus through me as I step into my EVA suit and snap my helmet over my face. And then I'm following the three of them through the airlock, into the unknown.

Minka leads us north, walking so swiftly and easily through the low gravity that the three of us have to jog to keep up. My eyes dart across the monotonous rocky ice landscape, nerves coiling my stomach in knots as I brace for whatever is coming. Minka's still not talking, her only response to our questions is a quickening of her footsteps, and soon the only sound in my headset is of Jian's or Sydney's voice, urging us to come back. But we're too far gone now. And when Minka finally slows her pace and I realize where we are, my heart stops.

It's the drill site—where the ice has already begun to

thaw, quicker than expected. Tera didn't make it in time, and now it's too late. We've just opened the lid to a box that was supposed to remain locked.

I grab Leo's arm, pulling him back.

"We shouldn't be here," I say through gritted teeth. "This isn't Minka, not really—something's happened to her, changed her."

"We can't just leave her here," Leo whispers back.

"I know, but—"

I break off as Minka suddenly stops and crouches down in front of the crevasse of thawed ice. We follow her gaze, and I yelp as she pulls off her glove.

"What are you do—" Beckett cries while Leo lunges forward to stop her. But no one is as fast as she is in this moment. With just one step, she's out of their reach, running her bare hand across the ice. And suddenly, the crimson light I'd seen moving in the ground before reappears—slithering in tandem with her hand. If a shadow could glow, this would be it—only it's bigger than any shadow I've ever seen.

It doesn't end.

"Oh my God, oh my God," Beckett whispers, his face a mask of fear. And then, as the crimson bioluminescence lights the ice nearest my feet, I notice something new.

Burrowed into the ice at the edge of the crevasse is a swarm of thick, razor-sharp tentacles, protruding from spongy round sacs—as if a flock of Earth's sea anemones had morphed with jellyfish, creating a disfigured new breed. My breath leaves me at the sight.

"L-Leo. Look—"

Minka abruptly stands and reaches for her helmet with one hand, the other hand unfastening the latch. Leo and I scream her name, Beckett rushes to stop her, but she's already lifted it from her head, exposing herself to the punishing elements.

I fight the urge to vomit as I wait for the nightmare that I know is coming. In seconds, her skin will freeze as cold as Europa's surface, while her saliva and tears begin to boil. Blood will froth around her nose and mouth while the oxygen rushes from her lungs, cutting off all consciousness. She'll be dead in less than a minute, and there's nothing I can do.

But a minute goes by, and she is still standing there—unchanged except for her ghastly pale color. And that's when it hits me: the unthinkable answer that's been staring me in the face, ever since she reappeared in the Hab.

"She's been dead this entire time." I look at Leo in terror. "What if—what if when we die on Europa, after the RRB we've been taking, you become . . . one of them?"

Leo and Beckett stare at me in shock. And then, like a horror movie playing in slow motion, Minka unfastens her space suit and steps up to the edge of the crevasse. I hold my breath, gripping Leo's glove in mine. And then she steps off the brink, slipping into the frozen water, as Beckett runs up behind her and shouts her name.

The anemones' tentacles unfurl as soon as her body lands, while the surrounding cracked ice sheet begins to move. In one sickening moment, I realize just what that movement is: the massive bioluminescent creature pushing up against the ice, threatening to break through. The winding red glow below the ice is growing larger by the second—just like the shape-shifting bacteria from the *Pontus*.

Before I can formulate a single coherent thought, the anemones' tentacles find Beckett at the edge of the crevasse and close around him with stunning strength. The bioluminescence moves and twists toward him as the anemones pull him under, and that's when I realize—they are connected. Somehow, this larger-than-life creature glowing below the ice is controlling the alien anemones. And the level of intelligence implied by that means we don't stand a chance.

Leo and I stand frozen, paralyzed with shock by what we're seeing. And then, without warning, he springs into action, diving into the water after Beckett.

I can't move, can't breathe. All I know is that Leo can't die for him—he can't.

I lean over the edge of the ice, my eyes searching the crevasse for the two of them. That's when something bumps against my space suit, and I scramble backward in horror.

It's the body of Minka. Cold, blue, dead.

My scream turns into a sob just as I spot Leo rising to the surface, a barely conscious Beckett under his arm. But now an even bigger throng of alien anemones starts circling the two of them, like vultures with newfound prey. Leo will be gone in seconds, and I can't, *can't* let it happen.

Mind, don't fail me now. Think—think—think.

Snippets of conversations flash through my mind: Leo, telling me how he caught Dr. Wagner analyzing his DNA with musical code; Beckett revealing the truth about the DNA component of the scouting and selection process. The revelation that life might have originated on Europa, spreading to Earth via panspermia—and that a certain fraction of the human population still shares seeds of DNA with Europan life.

If the undersea extraterrestrials could somehow think of Leo as connected to them, then he—and Beckett—might be safe. But how . . . ?

The idea hits me like a bullet. I yank my life-support backpack off my shoulders, reaching inside for the backup RRB vials.

I pour the RRB across my suit, my helmet, as many vials as I can douse myself with in a minute. And then, with a deep breath and a silent prayer, I take the most terrifying step of my life—into the thawed ice.

I extend my gloved hands, holding my breath and biting the inside of my cheek to keep from crying out as I let the extraterrestrials detect my scent. If they can smell the RRB on me, then I should smell like Europa . . . like one of them. Something they don't need to attack.

I wait, holding my breath, unmoving, as the anemones circle around me. The closer they get, the more I can hear it—an eerie hum in a pitch no human could ever attempt to mimic. As foreign as the sound is, something about it gives me the strangest sense of déjà vu. That's when I remember the sound coming from Dot's AIOS screen the night I accessed my hacked data—this was it.

And now I see the crimson glow through the reflection in the ice, blazing toward me. I scramble backward, terror making me forget my plan. The behemoth lengthens even more as it slinks in my direction, and when it lurches up to the thawed ice, I catch my first glimpse of bloodred, scaly, mile-wide skin. It's worse than any nightmare I could have imagined.

Fear clenches me in a death grip, and I'm this close to passing out when Leo's voice breaks through my consciousness, screaming in my headset for me to get away. And I remember what I'm fighting for.

I hold still, waiting out the most interminable moments of my life, for my RRB-covered scent to register. And then, I gasp as the anemones' tentacles retract. The bioluminescent giant surrounding me suddenly turns, shifting direction. I don't know how long this reprieve will last—now is my chance.

I plod forward through the water, the RRB forming a shield around me as I close the distance to Leo and Beckett. But when I make it to an arm's length of them, I feel the jolt of something pulling me *down*. Is it one of the anemones, or something potentially worse lurking in the water? I try to shake loose, to fight it, but I've used up too much energy, and now there's nothing left.

I'm falling under, inching closer to Minka's lifeless body. I close my eyes, seeing my parents and my brother one last time. I see Leo's smile, the way it looks every time we pull back from a kiss.

And then a pair of arms grabs me around the waist and starts to swim, yanking me up to the surface. *It's him.* We're going to live. I relax my body, leaning against him, waiting for the relief. But when we reach the surface, and he pulls me forward over the ice crevasse, I'm in for a shock.

"You?" I stare at the face of Beckett beside me and then look frantically out at the water, where Leo is pushing his way past a tangle of anemones to reach us. "You helped me? I—I never would have expected that."

Beckett falls back against the ice, his whole body shuddering from the cold.

"And I never expected you to help me."

I hear a yell as Leo's gloves grip the edge of the crevasse. I scramble forward, adrenaline rushing back at the sight of the alien anemones, their tentacles clawing at his legs as he struggles to pull himself up and over the edge. My RRB trick only bought us a few moments.

Mustering all the strength I have left, I grab Leo's arms and pull him toward me, feeling my muscles rip at the force. He tumbles on top of me, choking and gasping behind his helmet, just as I hear Beckett yell, "Guys—guys!"

I follow his gaze and stifle a scream. Two of the anemone hybrids are dangling from Leo's boots, their guts exposed in their clear, jelly-like sacs. I swallow the bile rising in my throat as Leo shakes them off with a yelp. And then, landing on the rocky ice, their tentacles start to shudder and flail. The three of us watch, stunned into silence, as they lurch away from us, springing back into the crevasse.

"They can't breathe the air out here," I whisper. "These— these things can only survive in water or covered ice."

Leo reaches for me, our helmets nearly colliding as we hold each other. Beckett collapses beside us, and I quickly scan our vitals on my biomonitor. Our oxygen is running dangerously low.

I swipe my wrist monitor, praying it still works, and then radio Jian and Sydney to prepare the Hab with our medical supplies.

"What happened?" Sydney's terrified voice echoes through my earpiece. "None of you have been answering for the longest time, and we thought—we thought—"

"We're okay," I tell her. "At least, I think—I hope—we will be."

TWENTY-EIGHT

LEO

"LET ME GET THIS STRAIGHT." JIAN STARES AT THE THREE OF us, looking like he's aged a decade in the time we've been gone. "You're telling me that Minka is dead—*was* dead, when she came back to the Hab tonight? And there's murderous alien life under the ice, which means—it's only a matter of time before one of us is next?"

No one answers. Jian sinks into one of the built-in seats in the Hab's common room, a sterile, half-empty space that we never got a chance to unpack. I sit across from him between Naomi and Beckett, still shivering beneath the heavy blanket draped over my shoulders. Sydney paces between the three of us, monitoring our vitals while blinking back tears at every mention of Minka.

"I—I don't know if I'd call the extraterrestrials murderous," I speak up.

Beckett gives me an incredulous look.

"Um. Were you not just in the water fighting for your life along with me? You think Minka was killed by accident?"

"I think maybe their instinct was to attack because they felt threatened," I reply. "Imagine if those same alien beings showed up on Earth. How do you think we would all react? Wouldn't our armies do the same thing—try to wipe out the unknown to protect our species?" I glance at Beckett. "Just like our leaders instructed you to use a weapon against them?"

"That's different," he argues. "We're the intelligent species. Of course we would think about things like defending ourselves and protecting the human race. Those things are just . . ." He shudders. "They're all animal instinct, no intelligence."

"You don't know that, though," Naomi tells him. "I think Leo is right. It's only the unknown that led them to attack—which is why when I entered the water covered in bacteria from their world, even though I must have looked different from anything they'd seen before, the familiar scent kept me safe."

"So you think that—that was the purpose of the RRB all along?" Sydney asks, her eyes widening. "It wasn't so much about radiation shielding, but about making us similar to these . . . beings?"

"That had to be part of it. But there's something else

that protects us," Naomi says. "The surface. From what I saw, I don't think they can survive outside the water." She shudders. "They must have pulled Minka in somehow."

Jian lets out a long exhale.

"So we could be safe as long as we stay at ground level . . . but the whole point of this mission was for us to drill through the ice and terraform the air pockets between ice and ocean into habitable land. How are we supposed to do that now?"

"I think that's pretty obvious, isn't it?" Beckett speaks up, and we all turn to look at him. "It's time to bring out the drones."

My stomach clenches.

"I know what they did to Minka—what they almost did to us. But we're the intruders here." I look each of them in the eye. "There's no amount of fear that will convince me we have the right to hurt them."

"Or me." Naomi stands up, shaking the blanket off her shoulders. "Do you guys remember when Dev asked us why we each think we were chosen?"

"What does that have to do with anything?" Jian asks impatiently.

"I've had some time to think about it, and I realized— there *was* a deeper reason, beyond how well we did at space camp. I think it had everything to do with what Dr. Takumi and the general knew could happen on Europa." She takes a deep breath, the spark of discovery back in her eyes.

"Beckett is the obvious one. His background put him in

the sphere of influence from the beginning, and by having Beckett on the crew, they didn't have to entrust anyone else with their secrets." She turns her gaze on him. "And somehow they brainwashed you into being ready and willing to kill whatever we found here."

"No one brainwashed me," he retorts. "I mean, who wouldn't want to be the greatest war hero in the entire history of the human race? Once I defeat the ETs here and claim this world for us, that's exactly what I'll be. So of course I was up for the challenge. No one had to twist my arm."

"They just told you all of that," I point out, trading a knowing glance with Naomi. "Takumi and Sokolov knew exactly what to say."

Beckett starts sputtering a rebuttal, but Naomi is already moving on to Sydney.

"Out of all the finalists, Sydney was the one with experience in marine biology. She'd studied deep-sea gigantism—creatures like that nightmare we saw glowing under the ice." She shivers. "If anyone can figure out what makes these creatures tick, it's Sydney."

Naomi turns her gaze to Jian.

"And of course, with Cyb being used for something more sinister than just piloting, maybe they knew he wouldn't last the whole trip. So they needed the best pilot they could find to take over. You."

"And where do you fit into this theory?" Beckett challenges her.

"They obviously sent me here to shut me up about what

I uncovered back at training camp," Naomi acknowledges. "But beyond that . . . Well, I've been breaking codes since middle school. Maybe they figured I had a shot at cracking the biggest code of them all—the language of the extraterrestrials."

I draw in a sharp breath. If she's right . . . then this whole plot is so much bigger than us.

"And then there's Leo."

"I wouldn't be part of their theory," I remind her. "I wasn't chosen."

"But Greta chose you. And she was part of the initial selection team, back when she was working with the ISTC." Naomi lowers her voice. "Remember what you found out before you left Italy?"

It feels so long ago, it might as well be someone else's memory: the voice of the prime minister's daughter telling me, *They've been watching you for years.*

"My ability to hold my breath for so long underwater—they thought it could make me some kind of weapon," I murmur. "I never really understood what that meant, but . . ."

"Your ability is the same reason Greta was studying your DNA," Naomi continues, her words coming out in a rush as her hypothesis builds. "Panspermia spread alien DNA to our world, and I believe you, Leo Danieli, are in the slim percentage of people born with traces of that DNA in your body. That's why Greta singled you out from the beginning, and why you were always meant to be here—no matter what choice the mission leaders made."

Her words sear across my mind, and as they echo in my ears, I know . . . she's on to something.

"Okay well, I think we've done enough analyzing for one night," Beckett says, looking at Naomi sideways. "If what you say is true about us being safe on the surface, then I vote we try to finally get some real rest. We can get back to this whole debacle tomorrow—or whatever day it is when we wake up."

Jian is already nodding before Beckett finishes his sentence, clearly relieved at the thought of getting to pause this mind-bending conversation.

"Beckett's right. It can wait till tomorrow."

I can't tell whether I've been sleeping ten minutes or ten hours when I feel hands shaking me awake. My first instinct is to smile when I see that it's Naomi, her dark eyes peering down on me. But she doesn't smile back.

"Leo—Beckett's gone."

"What?" I sit up groggily. "Are you kidding me? He went out there again?"

"Jian just checked the camera feed from our lander, and Beckett was seen there an hour ago, carrying some type of equipment out of the ship. And he obviously didn't come back here with it."

I stare at her.

"You're thinking the same thing as me, aren't you?"

"He was never going to listen to us," Naomi says numbly.

"He's using the weapon."

I throw off my covers and jump out of bed.

"We can't let him."

Jian and Sydney insist on coming with us, but nobody speaks as we return to the scene of our hours-ago nightmare. We're bracing with every step, steeling ourselves for each terrifying unknown. And then, from yards away, we spot the unmistakable cylinder of a small submersible. It glides across the ice like a shark circling prey, and the four of us look at each other in horror.

"He—he wasn't lying," Sydney whispers.

A familiar figure walks beside the submersible, his back toward us as he steers its movements with a palm-size device. Beckett Wolfe looks somehow bigger and more menacing from here, under the light of Jupiter—like someone who wouldn't just make threats but would execute them in a heartbeat.

The mini-sub inches closer and closer to the crevasse of melted ice, and I break into a run, swiping at my wrist monitor to radio him.

"Beckett, stop—"

I'm too late. The submersible is lowering toward the water, a thick rope unfurling from its side. Beckett follows right behind, stripping down to a pressurized wet suit and diving mask before stepping off the ice, grabbing onto the rope like a tether as he descends with the sub. He doesn't look half as afraid as he should be, after what we just went through—and I realize his confidence is directly linked to the power of the weapon. Right now, his drones have him feeling invincible.

"Why is he going down with it?" Sydney asks behind me. "I thought the submersible was supposed to unleash the drones on its own—why would he ever risk going underwater again?"

"Because someone still needs to set up the submersible on the seafloor and determine the strike zone and targets," Jian says grimly. "The drones are timer-controlled, so Beckett will be out of there in plenty of time."

Listening to them talk, I realize what I must do, and I freeze up. A small voice reminds me that I don't have to be the hero, that I can stay safe up here—with Naomi.

But we didn't come all this way to a new world only to destroy it.

I pick up my pace before losing my nerve, letting the low gravity send me half flying toward the edge of the crevasse. My hands shake as I undo my space suit, revealing the pressurized wet suit underneath. Jian snaps into action, opening two vials of RRB and slathering the serum across my wetsuit. Naomi steps forward, her lip trembling as she fastens a chain around my neck. A vial hangs from it, like a macabre pendant.

"You're making jewelry now?" I try to joke, though I can barely manage a smile.

"The chain was my grandmother's," she says. I feel

something squeeze in my chest, knowing how much that means to her.

"I'll keep it safe," I tell her before lifting off my space helmet, leaving just a diver's oxygen mask to protect me from Europa's atmosphere.

"*Te voglio bene assai*," I hear her whisper in my headset, and I turn to drink in her face one last time, before I step off the edge and into the water.

My first thought, when I feel the punishing cold splash against my suit, is that the last time I did something like this, I was hoping to die. And now, on this other world, jumping into treacherous water is my attempt at protecting the living. It's like everything is upside down when you're no longer Earthbound.

I slip my head underwater, and the current pulls me down with startling force. I swim against it, following the shadow of the submersible, and that's when I hear the hum.

It's a sound that prickles the senses, a different tone and key than any voice or instrument I've ever heard. There's something almost hypnotic about it, and I start following the sound, just as Naomi's voice breaks through my earpiece.

"Something's coming," she says urgently. "We can hear it through your mask-cam, and the rhythm is speeding up slightly as it gets louder. I think it means they're on the move—"

But I'm on the move too, transfixed by the hum that's

creating vibrations in the water, like a chorus in my wake. It lures me forward even as the conscious part of me warns to be careful, to remember my purpose of stopping Beckett's attack before it starts. The sound is leading me somewhere, and I'm powerless to resist.

Something massive looms up ahead—it looks like a dark cloud blanketing the ocean. It grows as I swim toward it, stretching taller and wider, while the hum around me reaches a deafening pitch, drowning out the voices that I know are calling me from the surface. And then, through a flash of red light, I see what's making the sound—and what's climbing and skittering around the growing black cloud.

It's the alien anemones. But where before there were just a dozen, now there are hundreds.

I quickly press the flashlight on my wrist monitor, sending a beam through the water. And my stomach jolts as I see another face, pale and familiar, on the other side of the black cloud.

Beckett doesn't seem to notice me yet as he scans the water around us, no doubt checking where his drones could do the most damage. He studies the anemones, an idea forming in his eyes, and I speed forward, toward the underwater cloud.

"Black smokers!" Naomi shouts the same phrase three times in a row before I can make out what she's saying in my earpiece. "That cloud looks like black smokers—hydrothermal vents that lead to the deepest part of the oceans.

They're alive, Leo. *Watch out!*"

Across from me, Beckett readies his weapon, adjusting the submersible's position on the seafloor. There's only one way for me to get close enough to stop the destruction before it happens—but it means moving through the climbing, breathing fog.

I choke back a scream as I swim through the black smokers, feeling the fog respond to my touch. A flurry of bubbles rise from it, foreign particles crawl against my skin. A high-pitched, piercing tone rings in my ears, replacing the sound of my crewmates' voices, before my headset goes dead altogether. And then, with a shudder, I'm on the other side, next to Beckett. His eyes blaze at the sight of me.

"Don't do this," I plead with him, even though he's not wearing his communications cap and can't hear me. "This isn't how we make Europa our own. *Please*—"

I break off as the flash of red returns, and a spiraling shape materializes ahead. The massive bioluminescent snake is back, inching toward Beckett and me. Terror seizes my chest. I can't think, can't move, can't do anything but stare at the long, winding red scales circling us.

It's just another form of life, I tell myself over and over, until I feel my limbs start to move again. But Beckett is back at the submersible, his face wild with fear as he reaches inside, about to press the button that will send drones exploding out of the sub.

I hurtle forward, side-slamming Beckett with all the force I can underwater. As he tumbles backward, I swim up to the submersible, scanning the command screen and trying to make sense of the acronyms and symbols. Finally, I spot a red circle that looks similar enough to the ABORT key on the *WagnerOne*. I reach my hand through to press it . . .

A heavy weight smacks me in the chest, sending my body falling. It's Beckett, clocking me with his life support backpack. And then, just as I'm recovering my breath, I discover that I didn't succeed in stopping him after all. I watch it unfold like a horror movie in slow motion, as the first drone barrels out of the submersible, a heavy sphere of sizzling metals and chemicals. It's aiming straight for the red bioluminescence—but when the sea snake darts upward, the drone misses. It hits the black smokers instead, exploding into pieces and sending metals flying, chemicals seeping, into the black cloud.

Fumes start to rise. The hum goes quiet; the anemones start to wilt. But that's not all.

Two of the shards ricochet, slicing open Beckett's sleeve— and my diving mask. Beckett starts gasping and choking from the pressure change and exposure of his bare arm, while the remaining anemones surround him, clamping their tentacles down on his skin . . . as if they somehow understand what he just did to them. And I wonder if anyone can hear me screaming underwater. Beckett—the larger-than-life nemesis who I figured would always be there—is dead.

I reach up to touch my diving mask, my fingers tracing the jagged tear with my bare cheekbone behind it. How is it that we were both exposed to Europa's atmosphere and ocean pressure, but Beckett died instantly . . . while I'm still here?

The submersible rumbles, about to unleash a second drone, and my stomach seizes. I could try again to stop it—but I've got barely ten seconds.

I swim like I'm back in competition, racing through the cloud of debris and up to the submersible. My eyes find the ABORT button, and this time when I reach for it, I feel the pulse under my hand and know my command went through. Nothing—no one—else has to die here.

But when I look back up, I'm surrounded by the flashing red glow. Just as I hold out my hands in surrender, slimy wet scales catch me in a death grip. The scales tighten around my body, my throat, and I find myself praying to my parents, my sister, through what will likely be my last moments. *Please, don't let me go like this. Please.*

That's when I realize that we're starting to move. *Up.*

We move at such dizzying speed that my vision blurs, and I grab the sea snake's scales involuntarily, to keep from going flying. And as I look at this extraterrestrial skin I'm holding, I discover that it was never quite a snake. Along with amphibious skin, it has fins and a color that changes from red to yellow as we break the surface, a shape that bends with its surroundings. It's . . . extraordinary.

The extraterrestrial rears its head and then shakes me loose onto the ice, where I land in a heap.

I'm safe. I'm alive.

TWENTY-NINE

NAOMI

BEFORE WE CLIMB INTO THE ROVERS TO BEGIN THE FIRST OF many back-and-forth moving treks, Leo and I take one last walk, stopping just short of the field of ice spikes.

"All along, we thought the universe revolved around us," Leo says, looking out at the ice-covered ocean in wonder. "But it was never true."

"There was a whole symphony out there this whole time," I add. "And we were only just hearing one part."

He takes my gloved hand in his. "Do you want to hear the rest?"

I look up at him with a small smile. "I can't say I'm not afraid, but . . . yes."

EPILOGUE

SAM ARDALAN SITS IN DR. TAKUMI'S OFFICE, WATCHING WITH rapt attention the scene playing on the screen before them. It's his sister, Naomi, climbing out of a rover alongside Leo Danieli. Sam holds his breath as the two of them step onto the smooth, pale, undisturbed terrain of Agenor Linea.

"We made it," Naomi says, turning her face up to the sky: a darkness illuminated by Jupiter's brilliant colors.

"We made it," Leo echoes.

Sam inches forward in his seat, studying every sight on the screen. The inflatable habitat is already set up in the new location, and the canvas structure makes Sam think of a grand flag: waving their arrival to this formerly lifeless stretch of Europa.

"It's hard to believe that, after everything we've been through, this part of the journey is just beginning," he hears Naomi saying quietly. "It's not about getting there any-more—it's seeing if we can terraform this world. If we can make it safe and fertile enough for everyone else—for my family—to join us."

"It's going to be a while," Leo tells her gently.

"I know." She looks up at him, taking a deep breath. "But I have you."

"To the moon and back," Leo says with a smile.

And then the screen fizzles to static. Dr. Takumi stands up from behind his desk, a triumphant smile spreading across his face.

"There you have it. The four survivors passed the test."

"What test? What do you mean?" Sam frowns at the enigmatic man in front of him. He came to Houston for answers, but instead all he's found so far are more questions.

"Can we change the physiology of humans to adapt to any environment? Can the science that allowed Leo Danieli and your sister to survive the alien waters of Europa be used in a different way, to help the rest of us adapt to living on our changing Earth?" He raises an eyebrow at Sam. "Can we use this science to cure someone for whom traditional medicine has failed?"

"What are you saying?" Sam asks, his voice coming out louder than usual. "I thought the plan was to send humans from Earth to Europa as soon as it's terraformed—"

"Europa was the beginning of a larger, more universal goal," Dr. Takumi says smoothly. "One that could benefit you, in particular."

"But—but—how long will they be alone there?" Sam sputters.

Dr. Takumi lifts his shoulders, looking at Sam as though the answer should be obvious.

"However long we need them to be. As I said when you first arrived—we have a number of classified programs in place to help humans survive and thrive in this new chapter for our species. The progress of each program informs the others."

Sam's head is spinning. He sinks back into his seat, looking around suspiciously.

"What is this place, really? I know it's more than a training camp."

"You're right. This is the DARPA Deep Space Agency—where military defense meets space travel." Dr. Takumi's eyes glitter. "Welcome to the future."

ACKNOWLEDGMENTS

First and foremost to *you*, the reader: thank you, with all my heart, for coming on this journey with me! When I was writing *The Final Six*, I never could have imagined how many of you would connect so deeply with Naomi and Leo's story, and I am beyond grateful to everyone who has read, recommended, and even created amazing fan art (!!) about the book. Thank you for continuing on the ride with me to *The Life Below*—I hope it's just what you were waiting for! <3

To my guardian angel on this project, editor extraordinaire Alexandra Cooper: I appreciate you beyond words! Thank you for believing in and championing this series since the very beginning, for making my writing *so much better* with your brilliant editorial insights, and your kindness and understanding as I juggled new-mom and then toddler-mom life with our book schedules. You are the best of editors and the best of humans, and I feel so lucky that I get to work with you!

Many thanks to my amazing representation team at Gersh and Energy. Joe Veltre, thank you for making my publishing dreams come true and being the best agent an author could wish for! Brooklyn Weaver (aka Super Manager!), signing with you was the first big win for this series. Thank you for all those early brainstorming sessions that helped me get to the heart of the story, and for guiding my career with such savvy! Greg Pedicin and Lynn Fimberg, you are two of my favorite people, and I am so grateful for your support. (Screenplays for you coming up next!)

To the dream team at HarperTeen, starting with the incredible Rosemary Brosnan: thank you so much for your support and for the opportunity of a lifetime to publish with you! I've been blown away by everything Harper and the Epic Reads team have done for *The Final Six*, with special thanks to Cindy Hamilton, Sabrina Abballe, Olivia deLeon Russo, and everyone in publicity, sales, and marketing who's helped spread the word and given me such wonderful opportunities to connect with readers. Erin Fitzsimmons, Joel Tippie, and Molly Fehr, I already loved my cover for the first book, but you've somehow topped yourselves with this one! Thank you for designing my fave cover ever. And thank you to Alyssa Miele and Allison Weintraub, for all your help at every stage in the publishing process!

I'm enormously grateful to the Man Ed team for putting up with my eleventh-hour revisions and always finding room in the schedule—thank you, thank you, thank you, Kathryn Silsand, Mark Rifkin, and Josh Weiss!! You three are heroes, and I am incredibly thankful for all your hard work. Many thanks also to Kathryn and Veronica Ambrose for your sharp copyediting skills!

Thank you so much to Josh Bratman, producer and friend, and the first person who said yes to this series back in 2016. You changed my life in the process, and I'm forever grateful to you!! All my love to you, Alex, and the whole Bratman fam—you guys are truly family to me.

It's the biggest thrill to see this series translated in different languages around the world, thanks to Hannah Vaughn at Gersh, and Allison Cohen prior. To my foreign publishers: Ediciones del Nuevo Extremo, Jangada, Epsilon, Imagine YA, HarperCollins Italy, Jaguar, and Editura Art, I'm so honored to have my books in your countries!

Megan Beatie, dream publicist—thank you for all your help launching this series, and for bringing me so many amazing opportunities. Caitlin O'Brient Bauer, digital marketing maven, thank you for designing me the most gorgeous website, introducing me to all things #Bookstagram, and helping to make *The Final Six*'s launch a success! Crystal Patriarche and Keely Platte at BookSparks, thank you for joining the team and helping us spread the word far and wide!

To the four amazing authors who graced *The Final Six* with blurbs—Kendare Blake, Alyson Noël, Beth Revis, and Romina Russell—I'm still so blown away every time I see your quotes on the back cover!! Thank you for your kindness and generosity in reading and blurbing—it meant the world.

I've been so lucky to get to consult with brilliant science experts on this series, including my good friend Dr. Teresa

Segura. Thank you for helping me put the science in the science fiction, Teresa! ☺ Dr. Robert Pappalardo, it was a true bucket-list thrill to get to tour JPL with you and learn all about Europa from the expert himself—thank you so much!!

To my beautiful Iranian American community—I am so blown away by the way you rallied around me and helped support the *Final Six*'s book release! Special thanks to Mariam Khosravani (you are a hero!!) and the Iranian American Women Foundation, Ali Razi, the Farhang Foundation, Phillip & Josiane Cohanim, and Haleh Gabbay. I love you all!!

And now, to my family, who are the reason and the meaning behind everything I do . . .

Chris Robertiello, my love, best friend, husband, inspiration: I've written you into all of my love stories, and I am so grateful to be living in ours. <3 Thank you for being the most supportive husband and partner, and putting up with all my deadline days and nights! I couldn't do any of this without you—it's a true team effort, and you are my MVP. I love you forever.

Leo James, my everything: I wrote these books for you. I can't wait for you to one day read the adventures of the fictional Leo, and see my love for you—more than the whole wide world!—written in the pages. Thank you for making me the happiest mommy on earth!

My parents and best friends, Shon and ZaZa Saleh: there are no words big enough to thank you! I would be nowhere without your support and love. (Not to mention—these books would never get written without your incredible help with Leo!!) I don't know how I got so lucky with you two as my parents, but I will spend the rest of my life doing all I can to make you proud and earning it! <3

To Arian, the best big brother in the world: so much of who I am is because I was blessed to grow up alongside you. Thank you for bringing so much love, laughter, and creativity to my life! And of course, many thanks to you and Sai for giving me the best little niece!!

All my love and gratitude to my amazing family on both the Saleh and Madjidi sides, and my awesome Robertiello in-laws! To my angels, Papa, Mama Monir, and Honey, thank you for inspiring me every day.

Mia Antonelli, you're the best friend I could have wished for—thank you for cheering me on during all the deadlines and being such a great bestie.

To all the booksellers, librarians, and teachers out there who have recommended *The Final Six*, thank you so much for getting the book in readers' hands!

And if you're still with me now, reading this last page, thank *you!* I am so incredibly excited to share this new book with you.

Dreams become nightmares in this heart-racing sci-fi duology from Alexandra Monir.

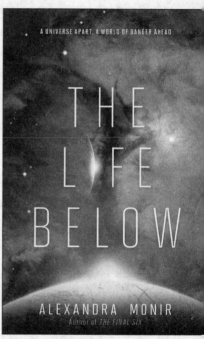